NEIL CAMPBELL is from Manchester. He has
appeared three times in *Best British Short Stories*,
and his debut novel *Sky Hooks* was published in 2016.
He has four collections of short stories published,
and two poetry chapbooks. Recent stories have
appeared in *The Lonely Crowd* and *Fictive Dream*.

Also by Neil Campbell

NOVELS
Sky Hooks (Salt 2017)
Zero Hours (Salt 2018)

SHORT STORIES
Broken Doll (Salt 2007)
Pictures from Hopper (Salt 2011)

NEIL CAMPBELL

LANYARDS

SALT

CROMER

PUBLISHED BY SALT PUBLISHING 2019

2 4 6 8 10 9 7 5 3 1

First published in Great Britain in 2019 by
Salt Publishing Ltd
12 Norwich Road, Cromer, Norfolk NR27 0AX United Kingdom

www.saltpublishing.com

Salt Publishing Limited Reg. No. 5293401

A CIP catalogue record for this book is available from the British Library

ISBN 978 1 78463 170 3 (Paperback edition)
ISBN 978 1 78463 171 0 (Electronic edition)

Typeset in Neacademia by Salt Publishing

Printed and bound in Great Britain by Clays Ltd, Elcograf S.p.A

for Naomi

I T HAD A silver frame and there was red padding over the handlebars with BMX written on in white letters. They'd got it from Asda. The spokes were sparkling and I didn't want to go outside and get the bike dirty. But my Dad sat me on it and pushed me off, and I cycled to Houghy's on Oakwood Avenue. Houghy was my best mate and came out on his Raleigh Burner and we tried the basic tricks of BMX like bunny hops and endos. Bunny hops were where you lifted both tyres off the ground, with your hands on the brakes, and hopped around. An endo was where you held the front brakes and leaned forward so that the back wheel went in the air. More than once we ended up on our arses. There were kids like Wisey who went to bike parks and did tricks on ramps. There was a place in Ashton-under-Lyne. But I was happy cycling around the Audenshaw streets. I had a sore arse for the first few days that's all. There was a footpath that ran past the end of my parents' back garden and we set up a jump on the path. Just a few bricks piled one on top of the other, and an old piece of wooden board resting against them for a ramp.

There was an old garden shed attached to the back of the house, made of the same bricks as the house and with a slanting slate roof. Inside it smelled of the linseed oil we used on cricket bats. There were shelves inside that my Dad had attached to the walls, and a little bench at waist height against the back wall. There was all kinds of stuff in there like tins of old paint, and all his tools in a plastic tool box that had different levels to it, and old jam jars with nails in them. There was a bag of sand on the floor and a tub of Polyfilla that was white with a blue lid. Houghy had gone in the shed when I opened it, put something in his pocket. He watched as I stood my bike up on its end and angled the bike into the corner of the shed before pushing the wooden door closed. There was a latch on the outside and a padlock with a tiny key. The lock was fiddly, but it closed properly. I forgot to ask what he put in his pocket, but I think that shed is where Houghy first got himself some glue.

The Dombovand's sweetshop was right near my primary school, close to Mandy Blackburn's house and just around the corner from where Wisey lived. Two-minute walk for them every morning, lucky sods.

It was summer, around the time of the World Cup. Me and Houghy went in the shop and after we came out and walked around the corner I stood there eating the Mars bar I'd paid for. He pulled a pile of football stickers out of his back pocket.

'You nicked them?' I asked.

'Piece of piss,' he said.

I couldn't believe it. A good fiver's worth.

'Your turn next time,' he said.

'Me? Well okay.'

Next time, I walked right in and with Houghy beside me stuffed a pile of the stickers in my back pocket. The woman behind the counter stared right at me as I did it. She didn't approach. Instead she appeared to phone someone, probably the school. Houghy said we should run but I walked back up to the counter and put the stickers down and ran out.

In school the next day I expected a bollocking but nobody said anything and I guessed they'd let me off.

Houghy approached me in the playground. 'Why did you grass me up at Dombovand's?'

'I never grassed you up.'

'Why did I get told off then?'

'I don't know.'

He kicked me in the shins. I kicked him in the balls. He grabbed me in a headlock and I punched him in the stomach. The dinner ladies stood around watching, and Mrs Burrows came and shouted at us. After fighting again at lunch, we were made to stand in silence next to the climbing frame, red faced and a bit embarrassed, while all around us everyone tucked into their school dinners. I looked at some of the plates and bowls: some had coleslaw, some sloppy mashed potato, some purple yoghurt, some semolina.

Me and Houghy went to Audenshaw High School and would go and get our hair cut at a place called Snips. From Hazel Street we cut through behind the Pack Horse, going down Poplar Street and coming out on Guide Lane past Hooley Hill. Then we walked up the hill past where the Junction pub used to be, past the ticket office for Guide Bridge train station, past the church and then right, beyond the Boundary pub and the Corpy Arms to the little shop on the main road to Ashton.

Most of the chairs were full and so only Houghy could sit down. I stood awkwardly behind the door and in front of the coats. There were newspapers on a table. Hairspray, shaving cream and condoms on the shelves in front of the mirrors. Hair in clumps on the floor. A framed picture on the wall advertising a gig for a band called The Paris Angels.

I looked into the mirror at the bloke getting his haircut and he was staring at me. There was this other bloke that Houghy pointed out. He was in the far chair getting his hair cut by the younger barber, Steve. And this bloke had about three strands of hair combed over, and he said to Steve, 'can you thin it out a bit on top?'

Houghy sat in Steve's chair and then finally Lawrence waved me over. I sat down in the warm leather chair and Lawrence started cranking it up so he wouldn't have to bend over. I always had to try and remember the exact words to say to him. But, did I wait for him to ask me or did I just say it? After he'd put the cape over me he just stood there looking in the mirror. I looked back.

'How would you like it?' asked Lawrence.

'All shaved off?'

'Sorry?' he said, pointing to his hearing aid.

'Shaved.'

'What number?'

'Eh?'

'What number do you want? Two, three or four?'

'Two.'

'What?'

'Two.'

'Okay,' he said.

I watched in the reflection as Houghy touched the point on his head where the stitches were. I felt a bit guilty. We'd been playing golf on the paddy fields a few weeks before and I'd accidentally hit him over the head with a golf club.

Lawrence was almost done when I heard Houghy moan in the other chair.

'Oh, sorry lad,' said Steve, having hit a stitch with the scissors.

The next morning it was pissing down as I walked along Stamford Road. I saw Houghy near the tuck shop. When I

4

went into my form room, the Old Chemistry Lab, the next morning, there was uproar. I did look quite different. I remember Mr Miller shaking his head at me and looking rueful. My hair was still wet from the rain and I ran my hands through it, spraying the lads next to me.

I remember a job we had to do when I worked in a warehouse. First, we had to scrub away all the pigeon shit. After that Rennie got the wide sweeping brush and pushed it all into one big heap. I bent over with the shovel and tipped it all into the battered metal bin. Then we lifted the bins onto the flatbed truck and wheeled it down the corner past the bogs and into the lift. Once down to the ground floor, I picked up the handle of the flat-bed truck, and with Rennie sat on the back, dragged the truck through the warehouse and out to the skip in the shadow of the MacDonald Hotel that was once the BT building on London Road.

For two days we went back to our normal warehouse tasks of picking and packing. Then the paint was finally delivered, along with rollers and brushes. The foreman said we had a maximum of two days to do it and that it wasn't the 'Sistine fucking chapel.'

We put on our new overalls. I used a screwdriver to flip back the lid of the first tin of paint, and as I did it, flicked some onto Rennie.

'You fucking prick,' he said.

'Sorry, mate.'

I poured the paint into the plastic frame and put the roller in and rolled it up and down, getting an even spread of paint on the wall.

'Fucking hell you don't have to fuck around, just get the

fucking paint on the wall. They've only given us this 'cos there's fuck all else to do,' said Rennie.

'Might as well do a proper job.'

'Fuck that. You make a start with that. I'll sort this fucking radio out.'

It was the kind of radio station where the DJ talks bollocks and there are adverts for local businesses, and the music is a mixture of smooth classics and contemporary shite.

'Hey, we could put the cricket on today. Test match,' I said, stretching up towards the ceiling with the roller.

'Nah, fuck that,' he said. 'You're dripping paint all over the place.'

'That's what we've got the overalls for.'

'You need to get the fucking extension on that.'

When Rennie went down the corridor to the toilets, I took off my gloves and started searching through the stations on the radio. Finally, I heard something good. I was hoping that the DJ hadn't said the name of the song before it started. He hadn't. He said it at the end. It was 'Factory' by Bruce Springsteen.

I was still sitting down when Rennie came back in.

'Break time, is it?' he said.

'Oh, you've had your shit now have you?'

'Nah, just read the paper.'

'Who put you in charge anyway?'

'One of us has to be. We need to get this done in two days.'

'You shouldn't go for a shit every hour then, should you?'

'We could drag this out, you know. Get a week out of it.'

'We'd get bollocked for that.'

When we'd finally finished we came back down to the ground floor with the empty paint pots on the back of the flat-bed truck.

'What do you want, a fucking round of applause? You could have had that done in a day if you ask me,' said the foreman.

'We just wanted to do a proper job,' I said.

'Proper job? There's more paint on your fucking overalls than there is on them walls. Dump those paint pots in the skip and then get back here.'

We did what we were told. It was warm outside, by the skip. But something in it stank so we came straight back.

'Can I just ask,' said Rennie to the foreman, who was sorting out deliveries for the following morning, 'what are we going to use the store room for anyway?'

'It is where we are going to keep the paint.'

'For painting what?'

'Well, store rooms, mainly.'

'What's the point of that?'

'Look . . . what's the point of anything? I'm busy. Just do what you're fucking told. You're getting paid, aren't you? Have your fucking break and then get back on picking and packing. We've got behind since you two took so long painting that fucking room. I told you it wasn't the Sistine fucking chapel. Fuck me they could have painted the Forth Bridge quicker than it took you two to paint that room. Anyway, look I've got a fucking monster coming through here from Trafford Park. I want you both on this Kellogg's one after.'

'Great job this, isn't it?' said Rennie, to me.

'What was that?' asked the foreman. 'Hey, you don't want this job you can go down the fucking road, sunbeam. There's still thirty fucking Polish I can call up today. And they're grafters. Not like you, fucking shower of shit.'

Years later, football career over and the warehouse job behind me, I was claiming Universal Credit. It had been a disaster for many people, the long wait before the first payment plunging them further into debt. People were saying it was like the Poll Tax, back in the 80's. If anything, I was slightly better off. But that didn't make it right. Every couple of weeks I'd take the short walk from my flat to the dole office on Wilmslow Road.

'I know I'm not who you normally see but Hafsa is on leave. So, it is me this week. Don't worry. So, what have you been doing?'

'All sorts,' I said.

'What is it you're looking for?'

'It's all on the form, chief.'

I had to show I'd spent thirty odd hours per week looking for work. I was supposed to do it as I went along. I put down two hours per day checking emails, job alerts from Indeed and CV Library, and then padded it out with other stuff.

'So, you've applied for a job in Leeds?'

'Yeah.'

'Long way that.'

'Can get a train.'

'Where in Leeds?'

'Near the centre. Says on the form.'

'I'm just double checking.'

'Right.'

'I don't want us to get off on the wrong foot.'

'Me neither.'

'I just need to look through this, you understand?'

'Yep.'

'It is Hafsa you normally see, isn't it? You said that, didn't you? Yes, she's on leave.'

'Yep.'

'Leeds . . . mmm . . . I'm from Hull.'

'Oh right.'

'Horrible place.'

'My brother's girlfriend is from Hull.'

'Well it's not so bad. Anyway, I'm from Kingston on Hull. Once choked on a battered sausage there.'

'Oh dear.'

'Oh dear, oh yes. Not recommended. So, anyway, you know we are here to help.'

'Yes.'

'Anything you need, just ask.'

'I will.'

'Yes, well that's all fine, so I will just fix you up for next time. You will be with Hafsa again, is that okay?'

'Great.'

'Any time you prefer?'

'About this time, if possible?'

'Just looked at that, already booked. Can do nine thirty? On the Friday?'

'Yep. If it's a Friday, I don't mind.'

'Okay. I've done that for you then now. I will just put it on your card.'

'Can I get one of the sheets as well?'

'Oh yes, here you go. See you now.'

'See you.'

'Take care.'

I tucked the blue appointment book and blank blue sheet

into my inside pocket, zipped my coat against the rain and continued down Wilmslow Road into Withington.

Ron was sat in the corner of Fuel, as usual.

'You having a beer?' I said to him.

'Oh, go on then,' he answered.

When I came back I saw the pile of books on the table. Beat poets, some of the lesser known ones: Diane Di Prima, Lenora Kandel, Kenneth Patchen, Annie Waldman. And his notebook was open, freshly scrawled poems filling whole pages of the A4 spiral bound pad.

'Just been at the job centre. Anyway, that's that done for a fortnight,' I said.

'Don't start me on them. You know they are trying to throw me out again now, don't you? Thirty years I've been there.'

'Seems out of order.'

'Bang out of order. There's been a definite change in them. They've tried the softly, softly approach. That didn't work. Now they are coming down hard. They aren't being nice anymore.'

'Why have they changed?'

'They want the house, don't they? They want to put a family in it.'

'Oh right.'

'It still has all the things they put in for my Mum and Dad like the ramp and the stairlift and the walk-in bath. So, I can see what they mean, but I've asked them to move me and they didn't come up with anything. They are just trying to evict me now. Court order and everything hanging over my head.'

'Sounds like a pain.'

'I'm starting to look at everything in a new light. You

know when they got me that skip, said it was to help me tidy up, well, it was because they wanted me to do all the work, didn't they? Now I've cleaned it up, well, now that you and Bill helped me clean it up, they want to get someone in. They say I need to pay six hundred by next week.'

'That's harsh. How have you got so behind?'

'Well, it's like I told you, there has been a change. I always used to be able to pay them when I had the money, now they want it in advance.'

'I thought everyone had to do that?'

'Well, yeah, most people do, but I didn't have to.'

His left cheek had started twitching. It happened when he got stressed.

'Right.'

'For years I've paid them that way. But now they want it up front. Six hundred and odd. Two months.'

'Sounds bad.'

'It is, but anyway forget all that.'

Soon enough people started turning up for Haiku Club. Ron put it on every week, free of charge. Sometimes loads turned up, sometimes it was just me and Bill.

The hardest thing was to keep the language spare, minimal. There were some newcomers, and everyone shared their work. The work of the newcomers was awful, they missed the point and couldn't avoid explaining everything.

When I went through his friends list on Facebook and began to private message them about Ron's situation, they all responded the same way. They told me how good Ron had been to them over the years, what he had done for them. I gave them his bank details.

After Haiku Club, Ron began telling me about his Mum

and Dad, how he cared for them. He needed to share it.

'I always had to kip with one eye open in case they needed anything in the night. I was always up in the night, doing something for them. But that's okay. I was saving the government thousands. So, I still kip on the couch. I don't seem to need much nowadays. I go on the X Box or watch DVD's. I got respite two afternoons a week. Bill came to look after them, as you know. And I came in here. Had a few bottles of lager. People knew where I was. Tuesday and Thursday afternoons, I was in the boozer, but come six I was in a cab home. Makes me laugh, the way Bill moaned at me sometimes if I was a bit late. All he had to do was sit there and watch telly. My old man didn't like him though. My Dad liked a chat. He was a hell of a talker, talk the hind legs off a donkey. But Bill, he's one of them just sits there has nothing to say. And you know Bill, he's a great guy, beautiful heart. But my old man didn't like that he was so quiet. He said to me, 'he's a bit odd that Bill, something not right about him.' You know my old man used to work as a weaver in the mills? He would cycle all the way to Manchester to meet my Mum. And then he had this heart attack in his thirties. Cut him down. Loved his cheese too. He would just sit there chewing through a big block of cheese. I always said, when they've gone, I'm going. Far away. I'm never doing care work again, I can tell you that. I don't mind wiping the arses of my own family but not a stranger's. When I was a kid, Mum and Dad took me to Wales. I always said I was going to move to Wales. Wasn't fussed where. Just somewhere quiet. Near Cadair Idris maybe, or the slopes of Tryfan, or the pig track going up Snowdon. Somewhere I could just sit and watch ravens, like my Dad used to. He was always telling me about the birds. And I know about those Welsh women. Ravens too. I knew a Welsh woman once. Seven sisters she had, seven. All with long black hair. When I was seeing her, it was like a fantasy, sat at that table with all those sisters. She used to beat me up in the end, so I had to leave her, but that's another story. I'm not getting into that. I moved back in with my Mum and Dad, and Dad had his heart attack and so that was that. Stuck with them forever. But it cut him down, I tell you.'

'Sorry to hear that.'

'When I was a kid it was before the airport. All there was in the sky was birds. You could walk out of here and it was fields. Mum would just kick me out in the morning and tell me to be back for tea. And she'd stand at the back door and shout me if I wasn't back on time. Sometimes me and Dad would go out for a little walk, Mum wasn't arsed about going out, it scared her going outside in the end. She'd rather stay in watching the telly, unless it was a trip to the doctor. Used to love that Dr Glennon. *Countdown* was the programme she liked, and she was good at it, got all the conundrums and that, which baffle me, I don't get them at all.'

'Me neither.'

'Yeah. Anyway, these walks. I pushed Dad's chair as far as I could, but we couldn't go that far really. The chair got stuck in the mud. They need to put something down so wheelchairs can be in the countryside. Anyway, we'd go as far as we could and then just look at the fields, and it was planes going over the whole time. Worse now. They get birds flying into the planes, the airport still has people to chase them away. You see them sometimes. They have recorded rook noises that they play at high volume from a speaker on top of a Land Rover. And then if that doesn't work they just run at the birds. I've seen these guys doing it. They get out of the Land Rover and just run at the birds, waving their arms, it's hilarious. Last time Dad saw it he was in stitches. He loved it though, getting out of the house, and I think that was another reason Mum didn't come. To give him some time alone. That's what she said. They bickered all the time when we were watching the telly. But they were inseparable really. In forty odd years of marriage they were never apart for a single night. That takes some doing. My Mum, she ate like a sparrow, and she was like this little sparrow of a person. She was tiny. Barely five feet tall, and when I needed to lift her she was light as a feather. My Mum was a feather, that's what she was. I lifted her once and it cracked her rib. That still breaks my heart. If you met me in the pub sometimes you might have thought I was pissed off looking after them all those years. Sometimes, you will have heard me say I wish they were dead. As a joke. I mean, I didn't have a choice, did I? My auntie went in a care home once and we visited her. She had a bruise on her arm and we didn't know where it had come from. And a necklace went missing out of her room. She'd only been there a fucking week. Asked us to get her out of there and we had to. I could never put Mum and Dad in a home. For some it's just Hobson's Choice, isn't it? I know that. Because I spent all my time looking after them, helping them with all their tablets and cooking for them and making them brews and lifting them out of their chairs for bed every night, and showering them and wiping them clean, and wiping their mouths too, and going up to comfort them in the night, and picking them up if they fell, and taking them to the doctors every week – my Mum needed to go every week, for a chat with that Dr Glennon as much as anything – and doing all that kind of stuff, I hadn't really got time to tidy the house that much, as you know. My Dad wouldn't throw anything away. The back bedroom upstairs, my old room, was filled with empty cardboard boxes. Well, you know, you saw them all. Whenever they bought something they just kept the box. I tried throwing some out once and Mum almost had tears in her eyes. She said Dad liked to keep empty boxes. She didn't understand why either, but she said if that's what he wanted to do let him do it. So, I stacked them all together. There was loads of stuff piled up in there. Even if I wanted to kip on my bed I couldn't get to it. But Wales was waiting for me, soon as they'd gone I thought I'd be there. They asked me to scatter their ashes in Wales. And I did that, and it was hard. But I can't afford to go back there. I don't have the money, I don't know anyone. So, what I thought I'd always do, didn't turn out that way. I was out the other day, doing a bit of shopping. And this woman says hello to me. People always let on to each other round here. And I didn't really recognize her. And then I realized something, she thought I was my Dad. I mean, I know I'm getting on a bit now, but she thought I was my Dad. They've all lost their marbles round here, I'm telling you. I went to the foodbank. They gave me another bag of sugar. Four bags of sugar I've got now, probably get diabetes in the end. Got some Jaffa cakes as well though. That will keep me going when the rapture comes, won't it? Ha ha. The woman there passed them to me, like it was a secret, a special treat.'

'You want another beer?' I asked.

'Yeah,' he said.

It was the usual mix at any spoken word night: misogynistic middle-aged white men, gay readers with poems about being gay, women reading about cats, but there was one reader there who came out with something a bit different. She was Chinese, but as she said in her introduction, she had been adopted and had lived in County Durham all her life. She was wearing a pink t-shirt that said, 'Token'. Her poems were about her experiences, whether that was people assuming she didn't speak English, or a policeman accusing her of selling illegal DVD's on Oxford Road, or of men attracted not to her but to her type.

'Hi,' I said to her afterwards. 'Cho, isn't it? I liked your Yellow Fever poem.'

'Oh, okay. Are you reading?' she asked.

'Yeah.'

'Great. I read at the Three Minute Theatre last week. I got locked in the toilet. It was totes hilare.'

'I've read there. At Stirred.'

'Right.'

'So, what did you read there, the Yellow Fever one?'

'I don't remember.'

'I liked that one.'

'You said. So, what are *you* reading?'

I showed her the copy of my second novel. 'A couple of extracts from this.'

'Are you confident?'

'Yes I am. I'm not a massive fan of readings. But I want more people to read my books.'

'Is it any good?'

'I think so.'

After the reading she wasn't there and when I got home, I wanted to message her on Facebook. But I held back, left it a couple of days. When I did contact her, she agreed to meet up. The weather forecast looked good for the weekend, so I suggested the Sunday afternoon.

I met her on the tram near to where she lived on Chorlton Road, and we got off at Sale Water Park. She was wearing a black t-shirt that said, 'Something Wicked This Way Comes' in white letters.

'You alright?' she asked.

'Yeah, not bad.'

'So anyway, I hate the outdoors.'

'Oh right, well we can do something else.'

'No, it's fine, really.'

We sat on a bench by the lake, looking at the water.

'My old boyfriend used to make me climb mountains in the Lake District.'

'Oh right.'

'I hated it.'

'Well we can just walk round.'

'Okay. Do you want to come for your tea after?'

'Okay then.'

We walked further around the lake. There were two ducks shagging and Cho laughed her head off. The park would have been okay if it wasn't for the roaring motorway and the electricity pylons. There was also a dickhead with a remote-controlled speedboat.

After getting back to hers she made me a lasagne, and then we sat on her couch drinking tea. The second time I went there she asked me to grate limes for cakes she was making. Coconut and lime cupcakes. Later we went upstairs to the single room she lived in and cleared all her stuff off the bed and got in it together. In the morning I had more cakes for breakfast, walked home with more in my coat pockets. For the next few months we shuttled between hers and mine, spending almost every night together. It turned out that she was mainly into theatre, not poetry, and hardly ever read novels.

It wasn't so much a play as scenes from different plays, and it worked well, they were like the stage equivalent of short stories. Cho had written one of them and I enjoyed it very much. Though she wasn't particularly happy about some of the acting it was a good night, and she fielded the interesting questions from the Q & A, at one point dragging things back to the work performed when some old fart went off on a tangent and started banging on about politics.

This was Oldham Coliseum. A cute little grey coloured repertory theatre on a side street opposite a dodgy looking pub and alongside an Indian Restaurant. They were going to move it to a better location in the centre of town but plans were cancelled by the cash strapped council.

We stopped for a bit of a chat afterwards as Cho wanted to thank the director. But soon the volume increased as the drinks flowed. At a certain point, things got a bit giddy, so we headed off.

There were tattooed people with walking sticks or in wheelchairs outside pubs, drinking and smoking. Bad karaoke blasted out of open doors, and there were new benches on the approach towards the shopping centre. There was a man sitting on one of them, talking to himself and staring at us, red-eyed.

We walked down a side street and onto a main road near the big new Sainsbury's and saw a tram approaching up the hill. Cho started running after it and I followed, trying to keep up with her. We got on at a sprint, then sat down to get our breath back. My bad knee was aching as I looked out of the window.

At Victoria, we got off and switched trams for Piccadilly, moving through the Corn Exchange and down by the side of Marks and Spencer, where the IRA bomb had gone off in a white van, years before. At Piccadilly, we waited twenty minutes for our train. We half-listened to the regular recorded announcements, and there was a new one we hadn't heard before. A woman with a Manchester accent spoke about reporting anything suspicious, and there was the tag-line: 'see it, say it, sorted.'

While we waited for our train, a policeman sprinted off through the doors and towards the centre of town. 'Probably some fight,' I said.

Finally, our train pulled in. Just before we set off, two teenage girls ran onto the train and sat near us. They were out of breath and looked terrified. I listened as one of them garbled into her phone.

'They just said get out of the centre of town . . . we will get a lift from Alderley. No, they just said get out of the centre of town . . . okay . . . love you,' she said, fear in her eyes, the phone shaking in her hand.

I shook my head at them. What were they so frightened about? Town wasn't that scary. These pampered middle-class fuckers needed to get out and about a bit more. Get a bit streetwise. In the ten minutes that we shared the train, I looked at their pale faces, and just before we got off at Heaton Chapel I saw the two girls hugging each other and crying.

We walked up the steep stairs out of the station and along Heaton Moor Road, past the Elizabethan and the big beer garden at the front, and then past the war memorial outside

St Paul's. Once inside we went straight to bed, and, in the morning, I took my arms from around Cho, got up and put on coffee and had some toast before switching on the TV. And there it was, the news of the terror attack at the Manchester Arena, where suicide bomber Salman Abedi killed twenty-two people and injured hundreds more.

Before Cho got up and sat beside me on the couch, I switched the TV over to an episode of *Dance Moms*. She would hear about the attack soon enough. She drank her tea and ate her Weetabix, with the usual piles of sugar, watching as the young girls were put through their paces by the dance teacher, their proud mums looking on. Cho had been a dancer when she was younger and had told me about the pressures involved. She still had a knackered ankle. After her breakfast, she got dressed and left for work, and I waved to her from the window.

A little later on, when I'd read more about the attack, at about the time that the flowers and tributes filled St Anne's Square, I realized that if we hadn't run for the tram in Oldham town centre, we would have had to get on the next tram, and this would have brought us right by the arena just as the bomb was going off.

A few days after that I took Cho to meet my Mum and Dad in Audenshaw. We walked down Lumb Lane from the tram stop, passed the old Ryecroft library long since closed, up and over the bridge across the canal and there it was on the left, the pitch I played on for Audi Rovers. The goals were still up at either end, but the grass was lush and green, even in the penalty areas, and there were no white lines.

Cho looked at her phone as I walked across the field. She

was addicted to social media. The motorway roared as I looked from one end of the pitch to the other, remembering how I scored from outside the area after Houghy had passed to me. On that same glorious day, I scored four before half-time, and six within the hour. I came off at the end, soaked to the skin, my hands tucked inside the sodden sleeves of the shirt. It was a white City away kit, the one David White scored four in at Aston Villa, but with the Audi Rovers badge sewn on it. Later that season I got picked for Tameside Boys, scored four, and was spotted by a City scout. After that I played for a team called Midas, who were known as a feeder team for City, and then played a few times for the youth team, including that fateful day when my knee fucked up.

'Bored now!' shouted Cho, from behind the goal where she stood with her arms folded and her hood up against the cold.

I jogged back to her and we carried on walking, through the gates, over the railway and under the motorway, past my old primary school, the church and the reservoir.

'Are we nearly there yet?' said Cho, sarcastically.

'Not far now,' I said, as we crossed Stamford Road. 'It will be fine, they will be more nervous than you.'

I was right, they were more nervous, but they liked her, even more so when I told them later that though she didn't like sea food, she'd eaten the prawn cocktail.

There was never any job in Leeds, but I did get an agency job as a learning support assistant at Arden College in North-enden. They'd had a massive enrolment and loads of students had support needs, more than ever before, and more than the existing staff could cope with. I didn't think I'd be qualified. Turned out nobody else really was either, they sorted your

DBS out and you just learned on the job. Thankfully, more than six years had passed and my caution for being drunk and disorderly was no longer on there.

When I got to the college the lady on reception gave me an orange lanyard with a card in it that said VISITOR. I put it around my neck and was shown upstairs.

All I did that day was shadow other members of staff, watching their interactions with students. It seemed the main thing was just to sit with the student, and if they had any problems you passed it on to the lecturer for them.

For the last lesson they put me in an art class. The lecturer looked like the cliché of an artist. He had rumpled curly hair, a ragged beard, massive bags under his eyes, wore a baggy woollen jumper with paint all over it and ripped jeans with ancient Doc Marten shoes. After giving up on a PowerPoint presentation he picked up a paintbrush and painted what he wanted the students to do. I was shadowing the support worker for a girl called Aurora and had been told that if Aurora had a red wristband on it meant she didn't want to speak.

After taking off my lanyard and leaving it on the empty reception desk at the end of the day, I went out through the revolving doors and took a short cut over the football pitch. Crows and seagulls probed the ground for worms. Cut grass covered the sides of my shoes as I walked out through the little metal gate in the shadow of Princess Parkway. There was a crowd waiting for the 101 and we piled on, heading quickly at first down the Parkway, through Chorlton, past Southern Cemetery where I saw a pink balloon flying from the corner of a gravestone. There were a few City greats buried in there, among them Malcolm Allison, the finest coach the club had ever had. Less nostalgically, the Yorkshire Ripper killed one of his two Manchester victims close by. We passed the McEwan's brewery near the big Asda in Hulme, the smell of the beer filling the bus where I sat on the warm seats at the back downstairs. In Moss Side we passed the house where Anthony Burgess had lived for a time as a boy and then further along went beneath the flyover of the Mancunian Way and cut down round the back of Oxford Road past the International Anthony Burgess Centre. I'd watched a two-part documentary on Burgess that had been aired at Christmas a few years before. It was a great film, there weren't enough like it on TV. There was another one on JG Ballard, focusing on his life in Surbiton, raising two kids after the death of his wife while at the same time writing wildly imaginative sci-fi and startlingly prophetic dystopian fiction. There was another good one on a guy called DBC Pierre who won the Booker prize with a decent book in the Kerouac vein.

The bus made its way back onto Oxford Road via the old red brick building of the Hotspur Press, and then the Rainbow Snooker Club and then The Ritz, before heading up towards Piccadilly. I got off near Princess Street and walked down past the Art gallery towards the library. There were Metrolink lines criss-crossing the road and a big square of open space that gave a great vantage point to see the library in all its revamped splendour. St Peter's Square, sight of the Peterloo Massacre two hundred years before, when the cavalry had killed some of the working-class protestors. I'd seen some decent writers reading in the library over the years, Irish short story writer Colin Barret among them, and had even read there myself alongside flash fiction maestro David Gaffney.

After nipping in to a Tesco Express and getting myself a

sandwich and a flapjack to tide me over, I thought about going for a pint. There were some lovely pubs and bars nearby that I had been in over the years. But I thought to myself to just go to the reading, enjoy the words, appreciate the fact of being able to see a great writer when most of the great writers were no longer around, writers I mostly discovered after they were long dead like John Fante. James Kelman was still around and in fine form and I thought I might get to see him one day, hoped to do so, he had become a hero of mine, especially through his short stories some of which reminded me of my warehouse days. I liked the ones where he didn't use too much dialogue, pure, Chekhov-style stories such as 'The Sunday Papers'. There was another one about council gardeners that I loved – intelligent men working menial jobs, given a voice by Kelman. I read Anthony Cartwright too, his Black Country novels about footballers and factory workers.

I still hadn't read all Knausgaard's *My Struggle* books but had enjoyed the first one enough to know that here was a great writer, a brave voice, an honest voice out of Bukowski, out of Kerouac, autobiographical fiction rather than the researched, plot-based, historical cobblers beloved of the middle-class gatekeepers.

I leafed through the copy of the book you got as part of the ticket price. It was a beautifully produced object, called *Autumn*, with artwork in it and short non-fiction pieces written for his daughter, and in their accumulation saying something to her, and us, about the world.

There were three middle aged women on the front row, drinking red wine. Knausgaard was half an hour late and sat down in a chair opposite the woman who was going to ask him questions, a lecturer from Manchester University. He began by standing up and reading a short section from the book. He barely raised his eyes from the sentences, and instead concentrated on the rhythm of the words.

He listened very carefully to questions from the lecturer and then the audience, answered them patiently and thoughtfully when he could, raised his hands in mock surrender when he couldn't. He was greyer than in the photos, his hair seemed on the verge of turning white. His full beard, stronger in growth on the chin than on the cheeks, was also going white. He was a big man, had played football, been a drinker.

In the queue for signing I found myself standing next to a bloke who worked in the bookshop at Home, the same guy who had been there when that shop had been in the Cornerhouse on Oxford Road. I used to go in and look through literary magazines like *Ambit* and *The Penniless Press* and he used to let me stand there and read them for ages. When my first book came out I took a copy in there for him and he stocked it, which he didn't have to do. I took him one copy in at a time over many months, no profit to me but my book was out there, that meant something. We got talking. He told me how he'd read all the Knausgaard books. He also told me how he was still making short films and had a real passion for it.

Jim had his book signed before me, and then it was my turn. I thanked Knausgaard for his writing, told him that I thought reading him improved my own work, and he made eye contact, seemed thankful.

Years before, when I worked in the warehouse, I made my own sandwiches, often in the darkness of the winter mornings. But I didn't want to take a lunch box on the bus with me, I was embarrassed by it, so I wrapped the sandwiches, which could be ham or cheese or just sandwich spread and stuffed them into the pocket of my jeans. After the journey down Ashton Old Road on the 219, I'd get off at the stop near the Star and Garter, walk downhill past the red brick walls of the old Mayfield Station and in through the yard, ducking under the half open shutter doors and into the cold hulk of the warehouse. Once inside I'd cut down the back of lockers filled with oily fixtures and fittings, then tug my carrier bag out of my jeans pocket and hang it up on an old-fashioned wooden coat stand.

At lunchtime I'd get a tea from the machine and sit down in one of several mix and match chairs discarded from the office and take a sarnie out of my carrier bag. It would be flattened, the ham or cheese or sandwich spread mulched into the bread, sometimes so much so that the outer side of the bread would have grease smudges on it, and I'd devour these sarnies in the cavernous warehouse, washing it down with two thirds of the cup of tea from the machine because I couldn't stomach the manky bit at the bottom.

Back in those days I'd sometimes go out for lunch, maybe to the bank to get money out, or to go to the butty shop, Andy's on London Road. There was a little mirror near the coat stand, and I'd look in that mirror to sort my hair out, make it neat and tidy before I walked into town. In those early days, clean shaven and with a side parting, often changing my jeans every day, I'd also change out of my steelies and into smarter shoes at lunchtime before going out, so that if you saw me in town you wouldn't know I worked in a warehouse. But after a few years working there, I had a scruffy beard, my hair was shaved like I'd had it that time in school, and I didn't bother changing my jeans every day. I worked in my coat so that and my jeans always had oil on them, and I wouldn't change out of my steelies either, and I'd sometimes just leave the high vis vest on.

I knew this guy, a poet called Ken, came straight after work to Ron's poetry night in Withington. He worked doing some god-awful job at St Mary's, so it wasn't manual labour, but he wore a high vis vest when he was on his bike, and when he came in the pub he just kept it on, and there were loads of guys around like that.

After the bomb all these people had tattoos of bees done on their arms in tribute to those that died. Murals went up in the Northern Quarter. Quite a while after that they started putting all these different coloured bee sculptures around the city. The Manchester worker bee, busy as a bee, hives of activity in the mills. I knew it from the Boddington's Brewery near Strangeways, but Boddie's had long gone bust and they didn't call the prison Strangeways any more. I wasn't against people having the bee tattooed on their arm in tribute to those that had died in the bomb attack, or the murals, that was a different thing, but the increasing use of bee symbols on bins and on billboards and then on these sculptures seemed like a load of crap to me. Working hard in the textile mills and all that, where you got paid a pittance and worked in fucking awful cramped conditions that made you deaf, while the owners of such places smoked cigars and lived in big fucking houses. That was the great myth that had always conned the working classes, all that shit about pride in hard work. Work smart, not hard, that was what I'd learned from lived experience. When you worked hard that was a way for them to control you. It had happened in all the jobs I'd ever had, all the jobs I had to take when my football career got ended by injury. In the warehouse they said I'd get a pay rise if I showed I worked hard. I worked hard and didn't get a pay rise. In the bookshop I worked for peanuts, same in the libraries, the post office, the colleges, and at busy times there was always a manager there, encouraging me, patting me on the back, those patronising twats. But they weren't stupid, they knew I thought they were cunts. In the end, when it came down to it, I always knew where I stood with them too: in the book shop the customers were more important, in the libraries the borrowers were more important, in the colleges the students were more important, and in the post office even the envelopes were more important. They tried to make you think that you were all in it together, but it was horseshit, especially on the zero hours contracts. Everyone was re-placeable and all the managers knew it. Even football was the same. When I had a good day people liked me, when I had a bad day they didn't. And when I got injured there was another young player in the pipeline to replace me. If you work too hard, particularly in the warehouses and factories, you are so knackered at the end of the day you don't have the energy to think, and so you get stuck there. You become an automaton, and that's the way they want you, they prey on the notion of working hard, that pride in working hard, and they prey on that to get the work out of you, but when you aren't financially viable any more they will take your sick pay, your holidays, your pensions, whatever they want, and in the end just fuck you off, and that's what I saw when I walked around town to see all these sculptures of the Manchester bee. The worker bee, the indomitable Manchester spirit. What a crock of shit. It was a marketing gimmick. Something for the tourists to take pictures of. And anyone who didn't work was less than human, and if you looked beyond the bees you saw more and more homeless every year, old men clawing imaginary spiders away from their face, red-faced women in doorways with sad-eyed dogs, kids zonked out of their minds on spice, the whole area around the concrete debacle of Piccadilly Gardens stinking of it. The Tories kept saying that there were more and more people in jobs than ever before. The truth was, there were more and more people in shit jobs than ever before, and the streets were filled with people who had no chance of work at all.

Back at the college, they put me with a student who'd been there for years. I reckon everyone who started there did a term with Frazzle. He was a big, shambling lad, my height but heavier, and when he got up off the floor in the corridor, where he sat waiting for me, it was like watching an elephant struggle from the ground.

The college had brought something in which they called 'The Agreement', a list of do's and don'ts that they tricked the students in to believing they had jointly come up with. Everyone had to wear a lanyard with their student ID attached. Another one of these rules, disguised as an agreement, said that all students would take off their caps in the class. Frazzle always wore a cap and said he had thirteen in total. He was shy, could hide under them. Although it was mentioned on Frazzle's file, the EHCP, that he could wear a cap, clearly none of the teachers had read it, and every one of them asked Frazzle to take it off.

Frazzle was doing Creative Media, as well as GCSE English and Maths. And it was all packed in to two and a half days. The Creative Media lecturer was a nice enough bloke, local lad, but he was a whizz on Photoshop, had been doing it for years, and didn't seem to realize he had to pitch things a bit lower for beginners. And week after week he asked Frazzle to take off his cap.

I learned from a previous support worker that Frazzle's main interests, aside from playing computer games all night, were history and horror. In an art class the previous year, he created his own designs for flags of the world, combining existing designs and creating flags for new countries conjured in his mind. I'd seen some of it on the walls in the art room.

The first project in Creative Media was to use Photoshop to do a poster, detailing 'The Agreement', and Frazzle's was one of the best, telling people to turn their phones off and incorporating a design from an edition of George Orwell's *1984*. It went up on the wall, and every time he said the work we did after that was 'futile' I pointed out his poster, and this cheered him up. The next project was to create a new version of Teletubbies for the adult market. For this he created a poster where Dipsy stood alone, dressed in black, cigarette in mouth, rifle in hand, knife taped to his bicep.

After a few months, I think when Frazzle came to realize I was on his side, he began to start conversations, even asking how I was. And sometimes he'd preface what he had to say, as we sat together at the desk, by leaning over and whispering, 'Fun Fact', before telling me something about the Roman emperor Hadrian or the lesser known works of horror director George A. Romero. One time he mentioned a Romero film called 'The Crazies' and said how it had 'many parallels with Trump's America'.

Another time, as I sat on a computer beside him before class, I showed him my website. When he saw I'd had some poems published he opened his notebook and showed me three poems he'd copied out. One was Frost's, 'The Road Not Taken'. He told me that Frost had written it for his friend, and this friend of Frost's had committed suicide.

Frazzle also said he sometimes wrote haiku. I showed him some online by Issa, a whole archive of Issa's poems. *The snail climbs up Mount Fuji – slowly, slowly.* That kind of thing. Frazzle seemed unimpressed, but a few weeks later referred to Issa's haiku about pissing in the snow.

The college accepted all students, at whatever time of the year, often kids who had been kicked out of other places. Student numbers meant more money for the college, and that was the bottom line. Every student had a diagnostic test at the start of the year to see where they were at, even if they had been there for years like Frazzle. Then it was practice tests and mock exams all the way, with very little time left for actual teaching. Frazzle hated having tests, and so, when we were asked to go to the library so that he could do an online test in either English or Maths, he pretended to not know how to log on, typing his password in wrong over and over.

One day he was stuffing a chocolate muffin in his mouth and washing it down with hot chocolate.

'Morning, Frazzle,' I said.

'Morning.'

'How are you?'

'I didn't sleep too well last night.'

'Oh.'

'Yeah, there was some confusion.'

'Were you up playing games all night?'

'No, I was not,' he said, a slight smile breaking from his lips.

'Okay. Well, it's Maths this morning.'

'Oh god.'

'Well, we'll get it out of the way.'

'Life is futile.'

'Yeah. I know what you mean. But just get the qualification and you'll never have to do Maths again.'

He finished his muffin and gulped down the last of the hot chocolate, putting the rubbish in the bin on the way to the desk, where we sat together. Today it would be about fractions. The lecturer did fifteen minutes at the start then gave everyone a worksheet and left them to it, just sitting at his computer doing the register, or putting together the next class, or nipping out to do photocopying.

Not having read Frazzle's file, but knowing he was a SEN student, this lecturer adapted by aiming specific questions at Frazzle, so that every week Frazzle was put on the spot in front of the rest of the class. I told the lecturer that maybe this wasn't a good idea but he ignored me and carried on the way he always had.

I sat there in classes, next to Frazzle, doing nothing except being on hand if he got stressed or needed something clarifying. If you sat there doing nothing, you were doing your job well. I'd worked that out early on, when I used to constantly ask Frazzle if he was okay. There was no need. I just had to sit there, be there for him, try to be his advocate to lecturers who didn't have time to consider how his needs might differ slightly from the others.

If you were assigned a student, you worked with that student, that was your job, and the more you kept your ego out of it the better. Otherwise the lecturers would have you doing more and more. They were on twice the money, yet half the time they wanted us to do their jobs for them.

I wasn't there to do photocopying or hand out pens, and if ever a lecturer dropped some folders on my desk I just ignored it.

We got through the Maths lesson. It didn't help the lecturer that they put students at different levels in the same class. Some were Level 1, some Level 2, so there were times when students knew that what the lecturer was saying wasn't relevant to them, and they switched off, messed about.

Frazzle kept his head down the whole time, cap pulled low, head tucked into his chest, often just scribbling drawings onto a little note pad he kept in the top pocket of his jacket. He would never look up from under the peak of his cap, but he was listening to everything – not always retaining it all, but always listening. I know he heard me suggesting to the Maths lecturer that he shouldn't ask Frazzle so many questions.

In the Functional Skills English class that afternoon, a lad about six foot five called Jordan rolled in with shopping bags, half an hour late, and then spent the rest of the time looking at his new trainers from every angle, ignoring the lecturer's pleas for him to do some work.

Frazzle had sighed when this big lad came in late, and kept sighing every time the class was disrupted, and I spoke to him over and over, trying to keep him calm and on task. At one point the lecturer came over to us. Her eyes were a little wild. I'd heard she'd had loads of extra classes dumped on her.

'What's going on over here?'

'We are just trying to get on with the work,' I said.

'Well, Sarfraz, I'm afraid we can't have you talking all the way through.'

Frazzle was taken aback by this, it was the other lad who was making the noise. But before Frazzle could articulate a reply she carried on, pointedly looking at me. 'It would be great if everyone had a support worker in this class, wouldn't it? But Sarfraz is the only one who has, so I would be grateful if you could keep the noise down to a minimum.'

I was about to explain to her that Frazzle was only getting upset because other students were being disruptive and making it difficult for him to concentrate, but she didn't want to hear it, and walked off to work with someone else. Frazzle couldn't understand why she had been so rude to him, but soon enough he seemed to forget it, and he smiled when she wrapped the class up half an hour early like always.

It was the next day when the manager of the Learning Support staff ushered me over and showed me an email from the lecturer, stating that I had undermined her authority and caused disruption by laughing and joking with Frazzle throughout the class, and that both I and Frazzle had been rude to her. She had also said she knew that Sarfraz was 'on the spectrum' but that didn't mean he was entitled to take over the class.

Around that time, I got some tutoring work, two hours per week. Ron had told me about this bloke called Brian, wanted help with his prose, would pay cash in hand. He lived in Heald Green, so I walked down to East Didsbury and got on the airport train for six minutes and then I was there. I walked up the steps and out onto the main road, planes passing overhead, and then got on Google maps to find the cul-de-sac where this bloke lived.

I rang the bell and the Superman tune played. His wife answered the door, a blonde lady covered in gold jewels. She led me in over the plush purple carpet and into the kitchen, where Brian was brewing up. He was a tall, slim guy, late sixties but looked about five years younger.

'You want a cup of tea?' he asked.

'Yes please.'

'So,' he said, 'I've googled you, no worries there. A bit of background about me. I published my first novel last year. Did it with Pegasus. You know them? Paid them two grand and they sorted it out. Then last year I sent them another one and they wanted to charge me five hundred to publish it but I said, no, I'm not paying any more. So, I've done two, but the wife says it needs more life to it. I'll tell you the plot: it starts in the ice age, where they've gone back in time, and their DNA gets moved forward to the present day and this girl, this bit's in contemporary Cheshire, she realizes her DNA is from the ice age and it goes from there. It is a very complex plot, but anyway I'm fine with plot, it's the sentences.'

'Okay well that's a relief,' I said. 'I hate plot.'

'Okay, yes, well, I will do you this tea and then I'll take you through and we can have a look at some of my writing.'

We walked into an adjoining room. It was at the back of the house, and as we sat there, aeroplanes crossed the window. He had a massive TV, and a big writing desk with the computer on it. He sat at the desk while I sat in a leather armchair.

'This is my man cave,' he said, before clicking on to Amazon and showing me his first novel.

'So, the thing is with me, I'm not from Manchester, I'm from near Wakefield originally but ended up here because I worked at Ferranti's. Ended up as a software engineer, started out as an engineer but ended up in computers. I was always quite creative in that job but at school I was rubbish at English. But once I retired I thought I need to have a go at doing something creative. So, I've been writing. I'm good at the plot, because I was always multi-tasking at work, but like I said in the email, there's something missing, needs a bit more colour, bit of description.'

'Well I can help you with that,' I said, passing him a sheet I'd photocopied for him to look at. It was the first page of the Turgenev story 'Bezhin Lea'.

'Oh, this is too much,'

'Well okay but that was just an extreme example to show you. Someone like Graham Greene might be better. He just does a descriptive little sentence here and there. Probably find some of his in the library, or Simenon, the Maigret stuff.'

'Okay, whatever. Do you want to look at some of my writing then?'

'Yes, that's a good idea, just print a page or two out and I will go through it.'

I looked through the chapter. I couldn't follow the plot, but most of the writing was fine. Short sentences that kept things moving, no grammatical problems. But there was a misogynistic lead character, and a lot of telling rather than showing. He wrote 'Trevor was bored.' I advised it might be better to say, 'Trevor yawned' or something like that. I made as much of the 'show don't tell' thing as I could because I needed the dosh.

At the end of the two hours he saw me out, and by the door we arranged the tutorial for the following week. I'd moaned a fair bit about the walk from the train station, and he suggested that we meet in The Gateway pub, near Parrswood.

The Gateway was a grand old place, rescued from closing by Wetherspoon's. It got a lot of passing traffic from the Parrswood Complex next door as well as all the old regulars from the East Didsbury estate. I sat with Brian and the pub was full of grumbling old farts, old boys with slicked back hair and heavy beer guts who nursed their ales and talked bollocks all night. There were no women in there, apart from the bar staff. The traffic roared by on Kingsway.

Brian's writing didn't need extra descriptive touches to make it better. The problem was that everything got slowed down by his lengthy descriptions of what his characters were thinking all the time, so I went through one of his extracts and just put a line through most of that stuff. I also suggested he might change it from third person narration to first person.

The following week he offered to buy me a pint. Then he offered to buy me something to eat, and I suggested I'd like the bangers and mash. Before he went to the bar to put our food order in he passed me something new. A short story written in the first person. It was by far the best thing I'd read of his. After lunch he said he was going to use the rest of his tutor hours to learn Spanish.

Cho's mum and dad picked us up from the train station, and we passed through Oswestry. There were a load of old pubs including a tiny one called The Fox, and curry houses and bookshops and cafés. We went around the back of the hotel, and after getting out of the car signed in and went up to our room, which was on the opposite side of the corridor to Cho's mum and dad. Cho was wearing a t-shirt that read, 'Hi, don't be racist, thanks.'

There were high ceilings and long sash windows with thick curtains hanging either side, and when you looked out of the window there was the great big church right there, across the other side of the busy road. Buses and lorries passed just below our first-floor window and it was cold, so we pulled the curtains shut before jumping on the bed and flicking on the telly.

The booklet said there was free use of the spa for guests, so we got up off the bed after just a few minutes and picked up a couple of towels and spare clothes and put them in a bag and headed over to the leisure area.

It was Friday, late afternoon, and we had the pool to ourselves. I gingerly walked down the steps and into the water, going in up to my chest and watching as Cho plunged in and streaked across to the other side using doggy paddle. At first it had looked like a panicked stroke, but I soon saw it wasn't, and Cho zoomed up and down the pool, seemingly without effort.

She went under the water and came up, her hair all glistening and wet, and we played around, held each other. Then we raced, and her languid breast stroke left me lagging. There was no splashing when she swam, whereas my swimming was just one long effort to avoid drowning. As I clung to the side, out of breath, she pulled down my shorts and swam away.

The wedding was to begin at half one the following day. After a leisurely breakfast we got dressed up, me in a dark blue suit I'd hardly ever worn, the trousers of which I'd had taken up at an odd little place in Stockport the week before, where a Polish lady with a loud voice stuck pins in the pants and then instructed me with grunts and points to put them back on as I stood there in my Reg Grundy's, and Cho in the dress she'd bought especially. She also put on high heels and make up, neither of which she usually wore.

The church was huge, mightily impressive with its stained-glass windows and sheer scale. When the vicar dropped the rings on the floor, it didn't seem a big deal, and he laughed it off. He was a curious character and I wondered how many weddings he had performed with this strange mix of expertise and incompetence.

The ceremony itself was quick and included a pitch perfect reading by Cho of a passage selected from the bible by her brother. Then there were an inordinate number of photographs taken, with various parts of the family snapped with the happy couple. By this time, Cho's new sister in law was finally relaxing, the sheer terror on her face as she walked down the aisle having faded.

We crossed back over the road to the hotel and enjoyed a meal that included some lovely smoked salmon, then went back up to our room for an hour or two in bed before coming down to the reception. The dancefloor was half empty but included a guardsman in full regalia. Cho's dad, an ex-army man himself, had said that if you put on a guardsman's uniform like that you had to wear it properly, couldn't even unbutton it, and so the guardsman kept on dancing the entire evening, through a whole load of tunes, from Elvis's *You Were Always on My Mind* to *Your Sex is on Fire* by Kings of Leon, sweat pouring from his forehead.

Cho got up and walked over to the dancefloor, started dancing, and then after a minute or two waved at me. I gulped down the rest of my Guinness and walked sheepishly over there, and when I started dancing she burst out laughing. I moved to leave the dancefloor and she grabbed hold of me, and we carried on dancing, me trying to copy her moves. When a ballad came on I held her in my arms and we did a sarcastic slow dance.

When Cho was on secondment in London, working as a script

reader at the National Theatre Studio, I went to visit her. It had been years since I'd been to London, a one-off visit, a day trip after a match. Cho was staying in Brixton, and when I got off the train at Euston I jumped on the bus. You just paid with your bank card, the driver never spoke to anyone, nobody spoke to anyone. I got off in Brixton, it was dark, and I struggled to find Cho's digs. She was just around the corner from the indoor market, and a train line went so near the house you could hear the rumble of it passing.

When Cho was in work I went in the Poetry Library on the fifth floor in the Royal Festival Hall. It was a cute little room with racks filled with every single author collection of poetry you could think of. I searched hard and found my own little chapbooks. They'd been kindly published by a rough arse cockney who set up his own press and worked his nuts off and got paid a mint by the Arts Council to keep it going. I visited him once, at his house on the wind-lashed plains of Newton-Le-Willows. It was a maelstrom of screaming budgies, feral daughters and groaning lurchers, but his Mrs made a quality spag bol.

There was a Scouse poet worked in the poetry library, divided his time between London and Liverpool and he was a great help in tracking down some Blaise Cendrars and Ron Padgett, then some Rimbaud and Patti Smith.

In the Ron Padgett book, I found the poems that had been in the Jim Jarmusch film, *Paterson*. A bus driver writes poems at night after his shift, thinks about those poems, gets inspiration for those poems while driving the bus. There were also mentions for William Carlos Williams, Allen Ginsberg and Frank O' Hara.

Filled with images from the poems I'd read, I started

writing some of my own, scribbled in the notebook I always carried. I wrote without thinking, just got it all down. Later, I'd go back to the notebooks and type some of those poems out. I had hundreds of them, rough around the edges, needed a polish that would come with the typing. But I'd learned not to tidy stuff up too much because you could take the life out that way. My influences had moved on a little from Bukowski too, and by now I was enjoying the likes of James Wright, Fred Voss and Jim Harrison.

In my early short stories, I'd tried to be minimal in a Raymond Carver type style, even if my stories were nothing like Carver's, and worked hard at polishing them up, taking out anything I thought superfluous to the story. But it had taken me a long time to realize that the writer's I enjoyed were not necessarily the ones whose writing mine would end up being like. I'd come full circle with my influences, getting lured dangerously close to academia in my reading of a critical work on James Kelman, instead of just reading the Kelman stories for myself and searching my own thoughts for meaning.

I was more attracted than ever to the rebels, the outsiders, the geniuses like Rimbaud and Blake and creators that came in their wake like Patti Smith, whose music I'd never got into but whose writing in books like *Just Kids* and *M Train* got my juices flowing and spoke to me much more about the creative process than any book on Creative Writing.

On my way out of the poetry library, I looked at a display about the Scouse poets of the sixties, and I wondered what had happened to all that rebellion in Roger McGough, a man now reduced to an affected radio voice on a programme that always destroyed any inclination I had towards poetry in the first seconds I heard it, a show that always just had poems by the great old dead white male poets everybody has heard a thousand times already.

On the way home, I went in a café near Euston Station. I got myself a coffee and tried to make it last while reading through my library copy of Knausgaard's *Dancing in the Dark*.

The coffee cup was empty and cold and there was still an hour to wait. I looked out through the windows and saw the rain coming down on huddled smokers outside the station. I looked at the menu board. I asked for a baguette with bacon, lettuce and tomato on, and the waitress said the only baguettes they had left were steak ones. I had one of those. With about quarter of an hour left for my train I asked for the bill. Fifteen quid for a coffee and a sandwich. I spent that on my weekly shop at Aldi.

Back in Manchester, my tenancy was up, and I was being asked to pay two hundred quid to sign a new tenancy agreement that would keep me there for a further six months, rather than on a rolling monthly basis. Because of this, and the expense involved in travelling back and forth from Cho's, I asked her if we could get our own place.

I loved Cho's face. I loved just to look at it, especially in bed when we gazed at each other all the time, pulling faces and mirroring each other. I loved the epicanthic fold in the corners of her eyes, the bright brown of those eyes, the symmetry of her nose, the long black hair falling around her face.

I wasn't hung up on Cho's being Chinese, she could have been from anywhere in the world and I would have loved her. I'd never thought of myself as fancying a Chinese girl before. Didn't even know about 'yellow fever'. But we had all this banter the whole time. She was well funny and took the piss out of me much better than I could out of her.

I was packing up boxes of books weeks in advance of the move, and when the day came I cycled to the Enterprise rental place on Burnage Lane, put the bike in the back and then drove back to Didsbury and started loading up the van. I'd been dreading it, all those boxes two floors up, but when I started I felt fit, carrying two boxes at a time as Cho sat in the back of the van minding the stuff. She wore a t-shirt that read, 'No Commercial Value.' A friend of hers came around and helped us out, carrying big bags filled with books. I'd run out of boxes so put them in carrier bags that cost 38p each from Aldi. After about two hours all my stuff was loaded up. Squeezed into the back of the van, packed tightly to avoid damage, and after going back up to hoover the flat and check all was clean and tidy so I'd get my deposit back, and taking the keys back to the estate agent at the set time, we headed off on the short drive to Heaton Moor.

As we started unloading, I saw Cho lifting heavy boxes and carrying two bags of books at a time. I was surprised by her strength. Her friend was now less enthusiastic, constantly stopping to stretch his back.

We still had to get Cho's stuff after that. She had been telling me for weeks that she had loads of stuff but looking around at the room she had in a shared house I figured there wasn't a great amount. I hadn't realized that the loft was filled with her stuff, and we were only just able to get it all into the back of the van.

As I parked the emptied van in the car park at the back of the flats, blackbirds seemed to quarrel in the dusk, their insistent calls crossing from one side of the garden to the other. I locked the van up, walked wearily across the car park and back into the flats, where Cho sat on the couch amongst piles of boxes and bags and coats and suitcases. She was smiling, happy. We fished out the kettle and the box of tea bags and had a brew, the last glow of the sun shining on the top branches of the trees beyond the car park.

After drinking the tea, we went into the bedroom and set about putting the bed together.

'Maybe we should leave this until tomorrow,' said Cho, 'just sleep on the mattress tonight.'

'No, let's get the bed done,' I said, gazing wearily at the page of instructions.

As I began separating out all the component parts of the bed it soon became clear that there were great gaps in the instructions. But I ploughed on.

I gave Cho a spare Allen key and we both worked at putting the base of the bed together. Then we attached the headboard. All was going well, even if it had gone past eleven at night. The window was open, the traffic on the busy main road had died down, the streets were silent as we kept on working.

It was an ottoman bed, great for storage because you could just lift one end up and store stuff under there. But attaching the levers and bolts and all that to the bed, for the mattress to lift, well, that was just too much for my tired brain.

Cho, a desperation creeping into her voice, kept asking me to leave it. But I wanted us to kip in our new bed on our first night in our new flat. 'I don't want to do this anymore!' she shouted, eventually. I turned and looked up at her from my prone position trying to sort the bed, and her eyes were blazing.

I put down the spanner and screws and went to hug her. She pushed me away. 'I wasn't ready to move,' she said, 'I didn't want to come here. I don't even know this place. This is horrid. I wish I had never moved. You're stupid.'

I felt awful. I'd been so focused on the bed.

'I want to go home,' she said.

'Well you've moved all your stuff here now,' I said, half joking.

'I don't care. I want to go home.'

'Look, I'm sorry. I'll leave the bed. We can sleep on the mattress.'

'I said that two hours ago! You didn't listen! You are so stupid!'

'I'm sorry,' I said, feeling panic, feeling sad, feeling like it would all be ruined unless I sorted things out right there, right now. I dragged boxes and bags, put them all in one corner, made room for the mattress. I found the bag with the pillows and mattress in and made the bed, all the time aware of Cho complaining in the background.

I went to the kitchen and made us some tea. When I came back into the bedroom she had climbed into bed and was lying right near the edge of it on her side. I climbed in, lay there on my side in the darkness. Despite the exhaustion, we were both awake for hours. Foxes shagged in the car park.

It was early the next morning. We lay together on the mattress. We'd barely exchanged a word. I lay there not knowing what was going to happen. Then she put her arms around me, tiny arms with the sharp elbows and strong little fists, and she lay there, her red-hot body clinging to mine.

I got up, left Cho snoring away. After making myself a coffee I put together the bookcase. And then I switched on the laptop and put the make and model of the bed into the YouTube search engine. There were two men in a shop in

Texas showing how to put an ottoman bed together. I watched the video. Paused it at certain points, rewound it, watched it again.

Cho really didn't want to help, but after she'd had two cups of tea we went back into the bedroom and tried to put the bed together again. What had seemed so impossible, in the fatigue of the previous evening, was now proving straightforward. When I was in doubt I just put the YouTube video on. The final bit was putting all the wooden slats in, and after we both did that I lowered the mattress onto them and put the covers on.

We climbed onto the bed, lay there, side by side. I saw a smile escape from the side of Cho's mouth. She wore a t-shirt that said, 'Drama Queen'. She climbed on top of me and looked me in the eye. 'I'm never putting furniture together with you again,' she said. 'You are insane. I told you to stop, and you didn't listen. You are insane.'

Later, the bedroom done, the kitchen sorted and only the living room to get right, we went to the takeaway. They had one of those Lucky Cats on the counter, waving its golden paw. We ordered Won Ton soup, prawn crackers, boiled rice, Dim Sum, got home and ate the lot.

After Cho put the dishes in the kitchen she came back into the living room with two cups of jasmine tea, which we made space for on the coffee table. As we sat on the couch, looking at a living room floor still filled with boxes and bags, Cho turned to me and said, with no trace of irony, 'I had to stay last night. Like you said, all my stuff is here. That's the only reason. Next time, when I tell you to stop doing something, you better stop. Or else I'm out of here. I'll hire a man and van, whatever. But I'll be gone.'

I got off the 370 before it turned left onto Palatine Road and walked down Barlow Moor Road to the college in Didsbury. It was half term. I went in to reception where they gave me a sticker with VISITOR written on, for security reasons, even though I told them I was already working for the college at the other campus. I was early, they said I could go to the canteen and get myself a drink. In the canteen there was a middle-aged woman and a young lad, shuffling about behind the counter, moving bits of bacon from one plate to another, straightening cups. I looked around the canteen: long benches before empty tables. In the far corner, two members of staff sat opposite each other, both looking at their phones.

Eventually, the manager I knew from Arden, a tall man with slicked back hair, a pinstripe suit and a daft little beard, who looked like Mr Toad from the *The Wind in the Willows*, came in and shook me warmly by the hand, smiled and said I should wait in reception now, as another candidate had arrived. They were still waiting for the others to turn up.

After a bit it seemed nobody else had turned up and so me and the other candidate got in the lift with the manager. He stank of sweat. On the second floor we got out of the lift and were led into a classroom, where another manager was there, a grinning woman with glasses I'd seen at Arden once or twice.

We were each logged onto a computer and taken through the assessment tasks. The first one was to punctuate a paragraph of prose. The second task was to listen to an audio recording of a university lecture and take notes. This was easy stuff, I waltzed through it, handed my paperwork back in, clicked to submit the online test. I looked over and the other candidate was still working away. He was red-faced, looked stressed, and I watched as he finally finished, puffing out his cheeks.

Then it was time for the interviews. I was happy for the other guy to go in first, and they said I'd have to wait for about half an hour.

An hour later I was still waiting in the room. I didn't mind. The longer it took the less time I'd have to work at the other campus later. I paced around, stood by the window and looked out. The roof of the canteen was covered in grass and weeds. I didn't know if it was some eco thing or just dilapidation. I could see the weathervane on top of the mosque on Burton Road, the mosque where Manchester lad Salman Abedi had gone. The mosque that denied they could have influenced him in a negative way. I watched magpies in tall trees. There was a jay too, I loved them. I looked down towards the car park. There were hardly any cars. I saw the manager down there, talking on his phone. What was he doing out there? Had he forgotten I was waiting? It was strange. The campus was strange. There was nobody around. All the computers were turned off.

Finally, the manager came in and ushered me through to the other room. I sat opposite him and his colleague, and they took turns in asking me questions, both very relaxed, both smiling.

Towards the end of the interview the female manager, Ally, said, 'So, I see from your C.V. that you're a writer.'

'That's right.'

'Have you published anything?'

'Yes, quite a few things.'

'Books?'

'Yes.'

'Do you make any *money* from it though?'

'Sometimes get paid for readings.'

'But the books don't make any *money*, do they?'

'Not really.'

She smiled and then carried on writing. Mr Toad then thanked me for attending, smiled and shook me warmly by the hand, saying they would be in touch the following day.

Two days later I still hadn't heard anything, so I emailed the manager. He replied that he'd forgotten all about it and would be in touch soon.

The call came the next morning. 'I'm sorry to be ringing with such disappointing news,' he said, 'but I'm afraid that in the end, after much careful consideration, we ultimately decided to give it to the other candidate.'

I was silent.

'I know this is disappointing. We just felt that in the interview you didn't say enough in your answers.'

'It is a bit disappointing. Especially since there was only one other person there.'

'Well, would it make any difference if there had been ten others?'

'Erm . . . guess not.'

'So, I'm sorry it is not more positive news.'

'I don't get it. I must have done well in the tests?'

'The tests, in this instance, were not the deciding factor.'

'Oh.'

'I think what it might have come down to in the end is that you are a victim of being an internal candidate.'

'What do you mean?'

'I think you have been a victim of being an internal candidate.'

'I don't understand. I think I'm just rubbish at interviews.'

'Well, like I say.'

'Although I did alright before, at Arden.'

'I know it is disappointing news.'

'It is so frustrating. Can I get more feedback?'

'Well there isn't . . . like I say, I know it is disappointing.'

I figured out what he meant a bit later. That stuff about being an 'internal candidate.' If they'd employed me on a permanent contract they would have had to pay the agency some compensation, what they called a 'transfer fee'. That could be as much as twenty percent of a year's salary. It made more sense for them to employ the other guy, who wasn't already working for the college, and keep me on a temporary contract. No wonder there were so many people working on temporary contracts. There had been no real point in me attending the interview and the fact that I was already working there was a disadvantage.

I couldn't be arsed going back to the college after that and started looking at all kinds of other jobs. Permanent jobs, ones where you got paid if you were off sick. Jobs where they couldn't just get rid of you whenever they wanted. Among them were driver vacancies for Stagecoach buses and the Manchester Metrolink. I sent in an application for one of the tram driver posts and was offered an interview.

I got the tram to Queen's Road, not thinking to watch the driver, instead staring out of the window at the lights of the city, where the red dots of cranes filled the skyline. I was reminded of *Paterson*. The central character, a poet, drives a bus, not a tram, all the time working on poems in his head.

But I had read what Kelman had done on bus driving, and there had also been that time I'd met a bus driver in a pub and he told me schoolkids threw cups of piss over him.

I signed a sheet at the security cabin and walked down the hill to the staff canteen, where I saw lots of overweight men in yellow shirts sitting around drinking tea and coffee. I overheard a couple of them talking, pointing over to a group of men not wearing yellow.

'Who are this lot?' one said.

'They are here for the psycho testing.'

'Again?'

'How many fucking drivers do we need?'

'Taking on loads aren't we. We need them.'

'They had seventeen in last week, didn't they?'

'I heard they didn't take any of those on.'

'Fuck's sake.'

I sat with the other men who didn't have uniforms, confirmed I was there for the test. We sat in silence and looked up at the TV. There was a news story about Donald Trump impersonating a disabled person.

We were sat there for ages, and I wondered if all the waiting was part of the test, or if the people doing the tests were just slow. We kept on watching TV, by now it was Dion Dublin on *Homes Under the Hammer*. I walked over to the machine, got a small plastic cup of PG Tips for 35p.

I looked around at the other men waiting. There was an Irish guy with silver hair and sideburns, looking just a little too relaxed. Then there was a younger bloke, wiry, with big hands, wore a smart grey suit and pointy black shoes buffed to a shine, looked a bit like the cage fighter Conor McGregor. This lad was constantly getting up and down to go to the toilet, and when he wasn't doing that he was telling everyone what he'd heard from a friend of his about the tests. As he spoke, he rubbed his big hands.

'My mate, he's been working on the trams for about a year, and he said it's a piece of piss. He said the written tests are the hard bit, and if you get through that they put you on the simulator and that's it. They also get you to climb in and out of the cab, daft as that sounds, some people can't do it. My mate says he was put on training a week after. They need the drivers, don't they? It's expanding all over . . . going to the Trafford Centre . . . and I think there's another one across town somewhere.'

'Stockport,' said the Irish bloke. 'There's one's going to Stockport, so they say.'

I looked around. There had been two blokes sitting together and chatting the whole time. And there was another bloke, sat at the back, his feet up on another chair. He'd read the paper, stared at his phone, been up and down for coffee from the machine. At various times other drivers came and sat with him, and they chatted away, but when the other drivers got up to begin their shifts, he just stayed there. The Irish bloke saw me looking puzzled.

'They're on standby,' he said.

'On what?'

'Standby. In case a driver calls in sick.'

'He's been sat there for hours.'

'Easy money, isn't it?'

'Suppose so, bit boring though.'

'Well, I'd rather be sat in here in the warm,' he said, smiling.

Finally, we were ushered into a room for the written test. The first bit was pictures of dials, which we had to put in order based on various instructions, and the second part was copying different shapes over and over, as quick as you could while the clock ran down. After that, we sat in the canteen for another couple of hours. Then the men came back in and three names were called, and those men left the room and didn't come back. The rest of us were told to get ourselves another brew.

After another half an hour or so, each of us was taken one at a time to do the climbing in and out of the cab, and to practice the announcements. When it was my turn I was given a high vis vest to put on, and we walked across the site to an empty tram. The man opened the doors and showed me the correct way to climb in and out. 'Obviously you could jump out,' the man said, 'but if someone sees you do that you will be in big trouble'. After climbing in again, I was given a sheet of paper with different scenarios. After reading the scenarios I chose what I thought was the simplest. I then pushed the little lever to one side, as I'd been shown to do, before making the announcement. The man sat in the tram making notes as I said, 'We will have a slight delay here. Someone has brought a bike onto the tram, and as you all know folks, bikes are not allowed on the trams. We will get this sorted out as soon as we can and then we can get moving.'

The man said that was perfect, very good, and we climbed down off the tram in the approved fashion and the man led me to the canteen. As we made our way back, I asked him if he had been a driver.

'Oh yeah, I was one of the first. On the Bury line. Did that for thirteen year. Then I started on the training.'

'How did you find the driving?'

'Oh, I loved it. You can just be in your own little bubble

the whole time.' That sounded good to me. When we reached the canteen, he took the high vis off me, and I went back inside, telling the others how easy it had been.

A little later we went to a room in a portacabin and were given a pen and a piece of paper each and told to describe our journey that morning in less than fifty words. The lad who looked like Conor McGregor had told everyone about this beforehand too. After that it was time for the simulator. We were led to a room in a portacabin with a handful of computers. There was a brief run through, and then we began on the simulator. It was like being on a computer game, except you were driving a tram from Rochdale town centre to the train station and back again. At various points we had to wait for the signal to proceed, and the other main thing to remember was that when you saw a speed sign, the tram needed to be going at that speed as it passed. It all seemed to have been explained a bit too briefly, but I didn't ask any questions when the opportunity arose, I felt too knackered, and after one practice run, it was time for the test. I thought I'd done okay but hadn't always been able to see the speed signs early enough. After the test, we all went back to the canteen. The two men were still there, chatting away, and the driver on standby was still sitting in the same place, looking at his phone.

They called my name first. They took me into a room that had once been the old control room. I saw a bank of screens all turned off, and a console desk, unmanned, with no chairs anywhere near it. After I sat down in a little office at the back, I was told that I had done well on the written test, they knew I was a writer and all that, and that everything else was fine, that I could get in and out of the cab okay, and that my announcements had been perfect, very clear. But unfortunately, I had failed on the simulator. I had been going too fast on multiple occasions. If this had happened just once they might have been able to overlook it, but it had happened four times, and so unfortunately, on this occasion, I had not been successful.

I avoided the canteen, walked out a different door and began walking up the hill towards the security cabin and the exit. I took out my phone, called Cho with the disappointing news. As I was talking I heard a voice from behind. It came from the driver's seat of a black 4x4.

'Do you work here?' said the man, unsmiling, grey haired, his head popping out of the window, a woman of similar age sitting beside him.

'What?'

'Do you work here?' said the man again.

'No, I've just been for an interview.'

'If you work here we have a no phone policy on site.'

'I've just been for an interview.'

'Put your phone away.'

'I've just told you I've been for an interview.'

'Put your phone away,' he said, smirking to the woman beside him.

'Oh, fuck off, dickhead,' I said, snapping.

'What's that? Right, I want your name,' he said, stopping the car.

'Who the fuck are you?'

'Doesn't matter who I am. I'm in charge here. What's your name?'

'Lionel.'

'What?'

'Lionel Messi.'

A car pulled up behind him, wanting to get out of the car park.

'Not the last you'll hear of this,' he said, crawling away in the 4x4.

'Go for it.'

'I said this won't be the last you hear.'

'So fucking what? Fucking power trip. Dickhead.'

'You'll see.'

'Oh, fuck off, dickhead,' I said, before signing out at the security cabin.

I'd written some long short stories and didn't realize how much they needed editing. I didn't write stories like the modern brigade, the middle-class ennui stuff that won the competitions. They didn't seem to understand the old Edgar Allen Poe dictum that everything should be in there for a reason, and they waffled on for page after page, much in the way Poe did.

I went back to the old books I loved, the ones that fired my imagination, works by the blue collar American writers that got me into literature in the first place: *On the Road*, *The Grapes of Wrath*, *Cannery Row*, so many Steinbeck books that I'd return to, but also *Cathedral*, *The Road to Los Angeles*, *Factotum*, and for my first foray back I picked up *The Grapes of Wrath*. There were bits in it that reminded me of that bloke at the Metrolink depot.

I'd furthered my love of literature through what were referred to as the small magazines, and before they did up the Central Library and got rid of them, there was a rack of mags up on the fourth floor. They had quirky names like *Iota* and *Staple* and *Bullet* and there were the local ones, *The Ugly*

Tree, Citizen 32, Rain Dog and *Brando's Hat*. Best of all was one called *Obsessed with Pipework*. Forget where it was based. After months of trying they published a poem of mine about a footballer with a bad knee.

Usually inside the back cover, or sometimes the front, these magazines had the 'Submission Guidelines' about what size fonts to use and how to format the work, and at first, I thought that stuff didn't matter, it was the quality of the poem that mattered, but nothing of mine got published until I started following those guidelines.

In those days, not everything was online like it is now. I had to print off my work and put it in an envelope with an s.a.e. I always remember going down in the lift from the council block I lived in at the time and walking over to the little red post box on Brunswick Street to post my little envelopes out into the world. Then I'd wait, weeks, months, sometimes even years, and each time letters came in the post I'd look for the ones with my own handwriting on. And when that *Iota* one came back with a little slip in it saying I'd been published, I felt like Arturo Bandini in *Ask the Dust* or Henry Chinaski in *Factotum*.

I had a shelf filled with the little magazines in which my poems and stories featured. I'd seen a picture of Charles Bukowski alongside a bookshelf where he had all the little magazines that had published him. Those were the days when I'd sit on the balcony of my council flat drinking Budweiser.

I'd seen things on Facebook where people said stuff like, 'I've had sixty poems published in fifty-two different magazines this year' and I'd think, what's the point of that? There was another thing where someone said they were aiming for one hundred rejections a year. What horse shit. It was my fault. I was connected to loads of writers through Facebook, most of whom I'd never met, but I was connected to them because I thought they might be able to help my writing in some way. One or two of them did. There was the editor of a great magazine based in Wales and he always accepted my short stories, and there was a woman who edited a flash fiction zine and I sent her some of my shortest stuff, and she put great photographs alongside them. A flash fiction guy from Northumberland too. But apart from them it was mainly people either trying to ingratiate themselves with their readership or plugging their workshops with *Ten Ways to Write a Short Story*, or *Twelve Great Ways to Start a Story*, or *Fifteen Ways to Sell Your Soul*, and these people were always either pontificating about literature of just generally waffling on about writing. I couldn't play that game. Being like that would put me off literature. There was a woman I saw at a reading. She seemed dead shy but the story wasn't bad. But the only things I ever read by her after that were things she said on social media. I wasn't connected to her but she kept popping up on my feed. Her calculated comments about what she called 'the writing life' made my blood run cold.

So many people just *love* being writers, especially those from comfortable backgrounds for whom being paid fuck all seems less important than having their *very own book*. The great writers don't tell you how to write, they spend all their effort and time on the books, because they know it is their books that will teach you how to write. But there were fucking freelancers all over the place, hawking their wares after getting one or two books published, and I couldn't stand their desperation. The kind of people who went on Twitter to tell you their worries about eating too much potato salad.

It was a continual campaign of canny ingratiation, and every time I clicked on to social media a little more spirit drained from my soul.

I wanted to read great literature and try to write great literature and the further away I could get from Creative Writing the better. It is an industry around writing that dilutes art and discourages the outsider, because you must come into the fold and shell out for an MA to ever have a chance of getting noticed. No working-class person can afford to pay that for a course that isn't even on a proper subject. And what did those classes produce? Conceited cretins who couldn't write, or clever fuckers who worked it out intellectually and had it all sussed out. It didn't matter that much to those writers what the actual book was about, so long as they were sure not to reveal anything of themselves. The whole premise of Creative Writing in academia is flawed anyway. They want you to show your working out, but good writing isn't maths, it's art. Questions, not answers.

I started reviewing short story collections for a literary zine. They didn't pay me, but I got collections of short stories for free. A proof copy of Denis Johnson's *The Largesse of the Sea Maiden* arrived. *Jesus's Son* had long been one of my favourite short story collections and I lapped up this new work. I'd never cared for his novels, the poetry of his sentences stretched laboriously across hundreds of pages, but his fragmentary short stories were marvellous and gave me the boost I needed. But I was getting bored of short stories. So many people seemed to be writing them to a formula and none of them stood out like Johnson's.

One day I was on my way back from the Co-Op and decided to go in the Children's Society bookshop near the crossroads in Heaton Moor. I'd picked up a few bargains before and was pleased to see an old Hunter S Thompson in there, a big thick white-spine Picador edition of *The Great Shark Hunt*, and when I got home I left the milk on the table and immediately got into the Thompson and it blew my mind in a way I'd hoped *Fear and Loathing in Las Vegas* would have when I read it a few years earlier. I still had that, an old second-hand Paladin version in faded orange with the Ralph Steadman sketches and odd underlining in biro by the previous crackpot owner. But this Picador one, *The Great Shark Hunt*, was a kind of 'best of' anthology and got beyond all that Gonzo, Raul Duke persona stuff, and I could see what the fuss was about – the actual writing. In some of its subject matter it made me think of the political situation in this country. Thompson's scathing stuff on Richard Nixon taken from his earlier book *Fear and Loathing on the Campaign Trail* showed Nixon to have such parallels with people like Michael Gove, Boris Johnson, and Jacob Rees-Mogg, those charismatic monsters of the Tory government who took the food from the mouths of children and gave tax cuts to their super rich friends while making out that the Labour leader was both Communist and anti-Semite. It was hard to discount the similarities between Thompson's nailed on thoughts about Tricky Dicky and the pencil thin fascist that was Rees-Mogg, and the whole name calling nonsense of the Tory government sickened me to the core, not because of their innate inhumanity so much as their ability to get good people to vote for them.

I both rushed through and savoured that Thompson book, and there were other gems in there too, a devastating character analysis of an ageing Muhammad Ali, that went beyond the simplistic hero worship of almost every other thing I'd ever read on the man, and a late effort called *Fear and Loathing in Elko*. I got on YouTube and watched some great films including one called *Buy the Ticket and Take the Ride*, but the best one was an old BBC edition of Omnibus where Thompson spoke about having a persona and you could see by his eyes he was a beautiful human being.

My mate Scoie had moved from Droylsden and into the Peak District, a little place between Whaley Bridge and Chinley called Buxworth. I'd known Scoie for ages, back when I worked at Manchester Fittings and he was at Tahiti Aquariums. My old mate Shackie only occasionally came out for a beer, happy as he was with his domestic life of wife and two children in a lovely house in Offerton, just outside the centre of Stockport and close to the Strawberry Gardens pub. Scoie had also got married. It was at Dukinfield registry office, and then off to a cracking do at El Sapo Perozo in Droylsden. His Mrs was also from Droylsden, and they'd been going out for years.

All his life Scoie had lived in Droylsden, growing up on Sandy Lane around the corner from Ashton Moss, before they ploughed up the green belt for cinemas and burger bars. His mum had died when we were at school, a big heart attack, and then he lost his dad a few years after that. He had an older brother, Harry, and when they stood there together with their shaved heads they looked like the Mitchell brothers off East Enders. They had season tickets together in the South Stand at City, and it was Harry's ticket I sometimes got for free when he missed the odd game to go on jaunts to London with his wife.

The train journey took me through Stockport and on towards Hazel Grove, and from Hazel Grove the views began to get more scenic, although just up from there a bypass was being built to ease congestion and churn up more greenbelt. We reached New Mills and went by the back of the Swizzels sweet factory and then to Disley, where loads of walkers got off, many of them clanking and banging the walking sticks that were supposed to save your knees but that just made you look daft and caused a racket.

They were all going to Lyme Park, the safe kind of country-side bordered by walls and fences and owned by the National Trust. And it was full of kids, always, and with all the surrounding green hills so many people chose to crowd together in Lyme Park, when the High Peak was just a couple more stops on, a place where you could walk all day without seeing anyone. It was visible from the windows of the train as I approached the high sided valley of Furness Vale and then still further, as I approached Whaley, and the green hills on the horizon were dotted with trees, and the clouds, shifting in the wind, left patterns of light and shade on drystone walls and on the slate roofs of outbuildings, illuminating the tiny white dots of scattered sheep on hillsides.

I got off the train at Whaley Bridge on a summer morning when the sun had already been up for hours and had warmed the old stone buildings. Near the takeaway hut outside the train station a group of brightly coloured, Lycra-clad cyclists shared banter while waiting for a few more middle-aged men with pot bellies and beards to join them. A couple of old blokes with rucksacks had got off the train, they had the old metal framed ones and wore ancient heavy leather boots and gaiters up to their knees. Traffic was slow through the village, going up past the White Hart and the Shepherd's Arms towards Chapel and Buxton, and the other way past

Kebabalicious and the big Tesco and joining up with the A6 through Furness Vale and back in the direction of Stockport. I had my Dark Peak map and followed a footpath Scoie had mentioned past the Goyt pub and the bridge above the river. I followed the glinting river for a stretch, and there were bits of trees in the water, big branches ripped off and caught up in something so they stuck there and the river splashed over them in white flashes, and the sun played on the surface, and the noise of it was there, unending as I skirted a muddy path by the back of a housing estate and then up a hill past an industrial unit and then a farm. At the farm I looked back and could see the scattered houses of Whaley that covered the big hill opposite on the other side of the valley, and I saw how it was in the High Peak, the valleys were the access routes. Along the valley floor you had the river, then the road, and then the train line, three routes running side by side along the valley floor, dating back to when the rivers were black and the buildings were blackened and the valleys were filled with smog. I followed the path beyond Silk Hill and came out at Bing's where the road reached a crest and the view opened above Buxworth and across to the bulk of Chinley Churn.

I dropped down the steep slope, the other side of Bings, and passed a road sign with a frog on it before skirting a bridge over the noisy A6 and reaching Western Lane. This was Buxworth, or 'Buggy' as the locals call it, a derivative of the original name Bugsworth. There had been a vote on the name, and just over fifty percent went for Buxworth. Scoie's house was at the far end, and I walked down the road, past the football pitch with its sloping goals and muddy penalty areas. The sight of the mud made my knee twinge. I imagined slogging through that thick turf, the claggy mud clinging to my boots, the ball constantly being blown by the wind, and then I thought of it after they put the netting on, and the sweet sound of that netting when a goal went in.

Scoie was ages sorting out his walking gear, but when he had we waved our goodbyes to his Mrs, who seemed pleased we were leaving. We headed out of his house and up the road leading past Portobello Farm, a vertical slog to the summit, from where we cut a corner across a field with a stunning view across the valley at Combs, above the reservoir and beyond to the grouse filled moors of Combs Moss, where cotton grass drifted in the wind.

We followed the road onwards and upwards under skies of quick-shifting clouds and floating jackdaws, and walked up to the summit of Eccles Pike, with the view across to Chinley Churn and beyond South Head towards Kinder Scout. The bass notes of ravens travelled on the wind as they spiralled through it playing, and there was a kestrel that Scoie pointed out, a brown pause in the sky. He passed me his binoculars, and I looked at the hawk's bright eyes.

We sat below the summit of Eccles Pike, on a bench, in the sunshine, the light of that sun sparkling on the distant reservoir.

'Fucking shagged, already,' said Scoie.

'Yeah, I can feel my knee, that's for sure.'

'Let's just sit here for a bit,' he said, taking out a flask and two plastic cups which he filled with tea.

'I never saw you living out here like this,' I said. 'How come you did it?'

'Well the Mrs has got family near here. High Lane, in Disley. That was part of it.'

'Oh right.'

'Yeah. But it's just chilled out around here, you know what I mean? You're out of the fucking rat race. And it's easy enough to just get on the train into town or to go to work so there's no mither.'

'Not much to do is there?'

'Well, all I really do these days is go walking. I'm going to get a dog I think, Jack Russell, probably. Just go walking. Fucking Droylsden these days, I mean, you don't get this kind of view, do you?'

'No, you don't.'

We sat there looking across at Coombs Moss, and then he said, out of the blue, 'I see they got Bennell.'

'Yeah. Fucking great news that. He'll die in prison.'

'Bit scary to know he brought some of them round here. Taxal, think it was, Furness Vale as well I think. Lived in Chapel. Could have been you that.'

'I was thinking that when I saw it on the news. But the coaches I had at City were fucking golden, do anything for you. And before that. Remember Audi Rovers? Norman, what a great guy he was, and a guy before that called Robby Kintyre, lived on Barn Grove. They were great guys, those that looked after us at Audi Rovers. Driving us all to the games. I remember when we'd pile in Norman's estate and he'd drive us up to Duki and we'd play Dukinfield Tigers. I always remember Duki Tigers. Can't remember other teams. Didn't you play for someone for a bit?'

'Yeah, Brendan Bees. Bloke called Brendan, funnily enough. He was a great bloke as well.'

'Oh yeah, remember now. And there was Boundary Park, from Oldham, they used to hammer us. Think Trevor Sinclair played for them at one point, and he ended up in the Premier

League. And there was a lad with a perm called Makin.'

'And there was Droylsden Youth and Droylsden Catholics, near me.'

'Oh yeah.'

'And Pine Villa.'

'Don't remember them.'

'Didn't they have a footpath going through the middle of the pitch?'

'That rings a bell. Failsworth Tigers, Chadderton Park, Gorton Juniors, it's all coming back now.'

'Oh yeah.'

I sat there, staring at the cotton grass on the hills across the valley, listening to the ravens, all the birds. How long ago it seemed, playing junior league football for Audi Rovers, on the ground beside the canal on Lumb Lane. I thought about Bennell, and what those lads had to live with.

After drinking the tea, we walked the long road back into Whaley, had three or four pints in the beer garden of the Shepherd's Arms and then crossed the road to Memories of India, where we enjoyed a curry before wandering back to Buggy in the darkness.

The next day Scoie drove us to the match. We sat high up at the back of the South Stand, in the cheapest seats. By now they were a Guardiola team, Pep had formed them into champions. From such height I could see the poetry of the passing, in particular watch the genius of Agüero, the way it seemed that the game slowed down for him, the way he always found space seemingly by doing nothing, and within minutes he had scored, like a dancer, *slow, slow, quick, quick, slow* as he took the ball almost in slow motion, rolled his foot over it quickly, lashed the ball into the bottom corner so that, in another slow motion moment, and in almost silence from the crowd, you could hear the rattle of the netting, and then the realization and then the roar, the roar for Agüero, and after the re-start came the song, 'Sergio, Sergio, Sergio, Sergio'. That song had love in it, not just for that goal but for two hundred plus goals, including the 94th minute one that won us the league, and one day City would let him go, but surely after that there would be a statue of Sergio, a statue depicting that winner, when he took off his shirt and whirled it around and the club was changed forever.

I watched again from on high as Agüero seemed to find space without trying and wondered how that could be coached, if it could be coached. The greatest players have that intuition, that seemingly natural awareness of how and when to move, and the goal-scorers also have that ability to find the net, the hardest skill in the game, that quality for which clubs pay millions. Whenever I went with Scoie I prayed Sergio was playing. Worth the admission fee alone, as they used to say.

After half term the agency got me some more learning support work. I had a day at Priestnall School in Heaton Moor, just around the corner from the flat. At reception, there was a screen where I signed in. The machine then took my picture and the man on reception printed it off and clipped it into the card holder of a blue lanyard.

One of the classes was for art, and the teacher had sent two lads, Ronan and Kai, to the back for talking too much, messing about. She asked me to sit with them in the far corner and gave me some pencils and paper.

'What's the point of this?' said Ronan. 'It's too difficult.'

'Take your time,' I said, showing him the start of my own drawing.

Ronan and Kai were talking about football and I asked them who they thought the best player in the world was. 'Has to be Messi or Ronaldo, doesn't it?'

'Ronaldo, Ronaldo, Ronaldo!' said Ronan. 'He was a United player and I support United.'

'What about you, Kai?'

'I think Messi.'

'No way!' said Ronan.

'Hey, come on, don't raise your voice. And remember, we're drawing.'

'What do you think, sir?'

'Well I'm a City fan, so I think Agüero.'

'Agüero? Be serious, sir.'

'Okay, so you say Ronaldo. Do you think he's always been that good?'

'What do you mean, sir?'

'I mean, do you think he was always that good? Was he that good when he was your age?'

'Well, obviously not.'

'So, how do you think he got better?'

'Because he practiced,' said Kai.

'That's right. And it's like that with drawing, you can't expect to be good straightaway. You need to practice.'

For a few minutes all I could hear was the sound of pencil on paper. My own drawing was coming along nicely. A decent pencil and good paper helped.

'What do you think, sir?' said Ronan.

'I think that's pretty good. Now have a go at something else. Try the clock on the wall.'

'Oh, I'm tired now, why do I have to draw something else?'

'Because there is still time left. What do you think of mine?' I asked, showing Ronan and Kai my drawing.

'That's really good,' said Kai.

'But you are too slow,' said Ronan.

'Too slow? It doesn't matter how long it takes. Kai, show me yours,' I said, and it was pretty good, and he started drawing the clock.

'Can't believe you are a City fan, sir,' said Ronan.

'Don't worry about that, carry on with your clock. Have a go at putting the numbers in now.'

'The circle isn't right though.'

'Proper artists can do perfect circles eventually,' I said, drawing a circle.

'That's not round, sir,' said Ronan. And he was right. Though I had improved with patience, the circle was not great. 'You have a go then, just on the other side of your sheet. Try a circle.'

Ronan tried the circles, noticeably improving until he got bored.

'Don't think about it,' I said, 'just let your hand go loose, fast and loose. Don't think about it. Just do it.'

Kai had finished his clock, and it was quite impressive, especially for a kid in year seven. The three of us spent the remaining minutes drawing circles.

After handing my lanyard in I walked home along Heaton Moor Road and went into the Moor Top for a swift pint. It was horrible in there, just set up for families and meals. But as I walked out through the beer garden I got a call offering me work at a college in Oldham the next day.

It was a bright purple building, I couldn't miss it. They

were a new academy, so it didn't seem to matter that I didn't have much experience. They were doing creative writing and as I'd so many books published the agency were sure I could handle it, even if I might have to take the whole class.

There was a fancy fingerprint recognition thing on the door. I'd never seen one before and faffed around before going back to the reception. Obviously, they didn't have my fingerprint. The receptionist opened the door for me. I went in. I could hear the noise growing as I neared the classroom. It was a nice room filled with colourful posters on the walls. There was a teacher in there so I supported him throughout the morning, looking at each student's work in turn and offering suggestions for improvement.

The afternoon was different. I was on my own, with no teacher, and no teaching materials had been left for me. I only heard later that the teacher had jacked it in that lunchtime. I just had to get on with it. I also didn't know how to get the whiteboard working. You wrote on it with a digital pen or something. After the kids saw me struggling to get that working I lost all authority. They started walking around the classroom, or worse, in and out of the classroom. At one point a lad I hadn't seen before came in and passed a package to another lad before accepting money in exchange. I tried to stop them, but I didn't know anybody's name and didn't even want to be a teacher.

I tried to get things back on track by setting them a written task, getting them to write something from their own experience, and some of them settled down to it. It's amazing how some students can stay quiet and get work done amid chaos. Just when I thought I had things under control I smelled burning. At first, I tried to ignore it but then I saw a flicker of flame from the corner of my eye and the lads all started laughing. One of the posters on the wall was burning bright orange and a lad sat there with a lighter in his hand flicking it on and off. A teacher from another class came in, quietly observed what was happening and then went for the principal, and when the principal came in one of the lads called him a cock.

There was an Irish lady in the staffroom. She wore a bright red dress and pearls and was very calm and relaxed. As I sat in the staffroom recovering she calmed me down by telling me how she was going to retire, how she'd bought a little cottage in the Wicklow hills.

She walked me back to the stupid fingerprint door thing and just before I left said, 'You were lucky. I wasn't going to tell you, but a chap last week got pinned to the floor by six of them and had his phone stolen.'

I told the agency I'd only do learning support after that. They apologized and said it had been a bit chaotic, it always was at this time of the year. Things went quiet for a while, then some learning support came up in Tameside.

Unlike at Arden, where I wore the VISITOR badge the whole time, the receptionist at Tameside College took my photo and said that later that day I'd get my name tag. Until then I'd have to wear a VISITOR badge on my green lanyard.

Tameside gave me a bit of background information on the student, something I'd never had at Arden. Because I was agency I didn't usually get to read this stuff, but Andrea, another member of staff, showed me Iffy's file. He was high functioning autistic, but it said that he had come from an abusive family, that the father was particularly violent, there had been physical violence that Iffy had both witnessed and been subject to and that sometimes, just sometimes, maybe once or twice per year, there was a possibility that he might wet himself.

I met up with him when the cab dropped him off and he wore what looked like a school uniform: black trousers and plain black shoes, a white shirt, and a blue tie that he had tucked inside his shirt.

'Aren't you cold?' I said.

'No, why?'

'It's freezing out there, where's your coat?'

'I don't have a coat,' he said, smiling.

'Okay well let's get up to your lesson.'

On the way up we bumped into Pete, another support worker who had been there for years and was known in the staff room as 'Mr Tameside.' He said he liked to stay down-stairs, rather than come up to the staff room, so that he could 'keep an eye on things' but really it was so that nobody knew where he was. Andrea said he did fuck all, but you had to have been there a while to spot that because he was a crafty sod. He did seem to rush around a lot, mainly out of the classrooms where he was supposed to be, sitting with students. He'd had some writing published, and he'd shown me one of his novels in the library. Some self-published cobblers about fairies and goblins. It was there on the shelf next to *The Canterbury Tales*.

'Hiya Iffy, I'm just sorting something out. You in Creative Media this morning?' said Pete.

'Yeah, we are,' I said, as Iffy hesitated.

'Okay well I'll see you in there.'

We were half an hour into the lesson before Pete came

back. He'd photocopied a handout onto green paper for a dyslexic student.

After the break we went in the English class. We had to do some creative writing as part of their GCSE. They had a picture of a park bench at night and they had to use that as the starting point for a story.

'Imagine that your character is in the park,' I said.

'What is my character?'

'You could imagine yourself in the park.'

'But I wouldn't be in a park at night.'

'Just imagine you are.'

'Why?'

'Well, for the exam, it's good practice for the exam.'

'I don't like exams.'

'Nobody does.'

'Why do we have to do them?'

'I don't know. For the government.'

'The government?'

'I don't know, look, just do what the teacher asked.'

'What did she ask?' he said.

'Look, you know what she said.'

'Right.'

'Imagine yourself in the park.'

'No, no, no. I'd rather not do that.'

'Imagine someone else then.'

'Who?'

'Anyone.'

'Pete,' he said.

'Pete?'

'Yeah Pete. We saw him before. He could get mugged in the park,' he said.

'I'm not sure that's a good idea.'

'I don't know then.'

'Well okay but change his name.'

'Really? Okay, okay then.'

'So, this will be in third person.'

'There's nobody else.'

'No, you know what I mean. Do you remember the difference between first person and third person?'

'Erm, no.'

'Yes, you do.'

'Oh, oh, yes, no, I remember.'

'Good.'

'Right then.'

'So, what's the difference?'

'Oh, right, yes, well . . . first person is when you use 'I'.'

'That's right. And third person?'

'You.'

'No, no.'

'Oh, no, it is when you give a name, when you use a name?'

'Okay so make a start then.'

'On what?'

'You know what.'

He started writing, covering up his sheet of paper as though someone might copy. After a couple of minutes, he stopped writing, and with his arm still concealing the paper from anyone around, ushered me confidentially over, to look at what he'd written. His handwriting was a huge scrawl, covering half the page.

Pete is walking in the park. He gets mugged. The End.

'Marvellous,' I said, causing him to laugh. 'But that's not enough.'

'It is half a page.'

'Only because your writing is so big.'

'It is still half a page.'

At the end of the day I went to reception where they had my new name badge ready. It was attached to a red lanyard. I exchanged it for the green one with the VISITOR badge on it, then put it into my pocket before walking out onto Beaufort Road. I made my way down Penny Meadow, down the hill and into the centre of Ashton. I passed by old pubs like The Bowling Green and The Prince of Orange, and the half-completed buildings left abandoned by the collapse of the construction firm Carillion.

When I got on the crowded 330 at what was now called the Station Interchange, I saw some people still wearing the lanyards they'd had to wear for work and wondered why they hadn't taken them off. We left the station, in the shadow of the giant *Ikea*, passed the swimming baths and headed out of Ashton past the library. In the seat opposite a man cradled a portable Roberts radio in its box and fell asleep. I'd heard him talking on the phone, he'd been back to the shop to get it repaired. Everyone on the bus seemed to be coughing, and the air conditioning roared out, spreading germs everywhere. The bus took forever to reach Stockport, winding its way through Dukinfield and Hyde and Woodley, before passing Pear Mill and making its way into the centre of Stockport.

The following week I was put in a class with a student doing Plumbing Theory. The lecturer looked familiar. It was Slogger Delaney, a guy I had gone to school with. His first name was Mike, and that's what the students called him. He'd got the Slogger nickname at school after a cricket match where we'd shared a fifty partnership that led us to victory.

He was talking to the lads about Health and Safety, how it had all changed since his early days in work. When he started off they never wore hard hats or high vis vests, and one day he was given the keys to a cherry picker. He'd never had any training. Another story was about him dislocating his shoulder, clinging on to a window ledge as the ladder fell away. He was a great teacher but it was so weird to see him standing there. Where had all the years gone?

During the break we went outside and chatted while he had a smoke. He sat on the bonnet of his Vauxhall Corsa and we had a good old moan about the college. We also talked about Houghy, our class mate who'd died while glue sniffing with a carrier bag over his head. Del's mate had found him and I hadn't known that.

After the break they did a test and I sat there, next to the student I was supporting, a lad called Luca. He told me that his mum had named him after the song by Suzanne Vega. He was dyslexic. I helped him spell some of the words but he didn't really need me that much. I just asked him about plumbing, of which I knew nothing.

As Luca plodded doggedly through the test my mind drifted back to school days, the fifty partnership with Del on the cricket pitch in the middle of the fields at Audi High, the cross-bat slog by Del, the winning runs, a big six that hit a car on Stamford Road. He was such a cool cat then, wasn't even that into cricket, just good at it. He wore a hat and carried a guitar, had an earring, played in bands, had girlfriends. I looked over at him, sat on the desk, resting the bad back he had told us about, made worse because of all the years not lifting properly, either because he didn't have the time or had never had the manual handling training. Del laughed when he told us stories about his plumbing days, smiled ruefully when talking about his aching back or frozen shoulder. There was no bitterness there, and I was gutted when he didn't come back after Christmas.

It was our anniversary and me and Cho went into town for a meal. After being shown to our table Cho wanted to see the lobsters. They were in glass tanks with their claws taped. We'd walked past them on the way in.

'Oh look, you can see their little black eyes,' she said.

'I'll take a picture,' I said, and she jokingly put on a worried face. When the flash came on, one of the lobsters shifted suddenly, Cho jumped, and we quickly sat back down.

Cho ordered the lobster roll and I ordered the 16oz burger. Although Cho really wanted to like lobster, after about five minutes she reluctantly swopped plates with me and tucked into the burger. On the way out, Cho wanted to look at the lobsters in their tank again, said how cute they were.

We walked back out onto King Street, holding hands as we made our way to the tram stop at Piccadilly Gardens. Just as we walked down Whitworth Street we walked past a group of middle-aged men in suits. I noticed a few of them looking at us. As we approached the tram stop, Cho turned and shouted, 'Your mate his racist! Look at him! He's racist!' And she stood there, sticking two fingers up at them.

'What was all that about?' I asked, watching the men as they walked away.

'*Love me long time.*'

'What?'

'Didn't you hear what he said? *Love me long time ten dollar.*'

'Oh, for fuck's sake. I didn't hear it, sorry.'

'Happens all the time.'

'Really?'

'Yes, it happens all the time.'

'Sorry. I didn't hear it.'

'You wouldn't.'

'What?'

'You're white,' she said.

'Oh, come on.'

'White privilege.'

Adopted from a Kowloon orphanage at the age of fifteen months and raised in County Durham, Cho was privately educated, had a master's degree, lived in England thirty years. We'd met at a poetry night in Manchester, not online. Even if we had met online, what was wrong with that? People are so quick to judge. What if she had lived all her life in China and just come to England to meet an English man? There was nothing wrong with that either. But this was the country where half the people had voted for Brexit.

We'd walk down the street and these perfectly nice looking middle-aged white men would shoot me a knowing look, and I smiled back at them because I knew they were stupid. The assumptions and presumptions they made in that moment showed them up as the racists they were. After a while it started to annoy me a little bit, the way those looks reduced us as a couple, reduced her as a human being. And I saw the way men looked at her body too, how that reduced her to a sex object, and I felt bad because I'd been that way about women as a younger man.

I borrowed a few books from Cho, one called *Everyday Sexism* and others called *The Good Immigrant* and *Why I No Longer Talk to White People about Race*. Everywhere I went with Cho she was usually the only non-white person in the room. It was a bit startling when I realized. Every person she ever met, that was what they saw about her first, and those books had things in that chimed with the stuff Cho had told me about. How people said to her, 'so, where are you from?' and when she replied 'Durham' they'd ask, 'no, where are you *really* from?'

After the *love me long time* thing we got on the tram, and it took us the short distance back to Piccadilly where we got on the 9.47 Buxton train, and got off at Heaton Chapel.

'Oh, Mr Writer, so nice to be with you. Here is much better than China,' said Cho, putting on a fake Chinese accent that covered her perfect RP. The lad getting off the train looked around.

'He has the yellow fever,' she said, pointing at him so that the lad looked embarrassed and turned away.

Cho started taking me to the theatre, said it would broaden my horizons. The one at Hope Mill was near the old Bank of England pub in Ancoats. That used to be well rough, and it still looked a bit sketchy round there. I held tightly to Cho's hand, keeping my eyes open as we walked the short distance from the tram stop. Not long before the police had found a body in that boozer. There was snow in the air and black ice on the roads.

They had done a good job converting the mill and there was a nice bar area, and before we went in I picked up one of the blankets for Cho, and she covered her legs with it for the entirety of the play. There were three actors that had been in Coronation Street, and a couple more TV people in attendance. It was a story about a bored middle-class house-wife and I fell asleep.

As we walked quickly back to the tram stop at what was now called New Islington, I looked back and saw the glinting lights of the Etihad Stadium in the distance. I looked at my phone and checked the scores. City had won, and another league title seemed a formality.

Another time we went to the Viaduct Theatre at the Hat Museum in Stockport. They said the hat museum was why everyone in Stockport was bonkers. Before environmentalism and all that, the mercury used to get in the drinking water, and that's where they'd got the phrase 'mad as a hatter.'

As we sat in the café by the windows you could look out across to the viaduct that took trains into and out of Stockport, high above the bus station and the centre of town. It looked majestic, the weak spring sunlight on red bricks as the trains tootled above. The week before a man had spent twenty-two hours on the ledge, drinking beer and causing train chaos.

There was this other theatre we went to, under the railway arches in the shadow of the Beetham Tower. Something for the Manchester Fringe. Cho was reviewing it for a writing prize. The acting was good but the play itself was about an actor berating himself for having been a bully at school. There was nothing about the kid who'd been bullied, and the writing was full of banal references to Facebook and Twitter and how we use mobile phones. I was surprised when it was given a standing ovation at the end. Cho blurted out, 'Well, I bet my plays would get a standing ovation if I had this many friends!' Three women alongside us all shook their heads after Cho said it. One of the women, stern-faced, asked Cho who she was reviewing for, and when Cho told her, this woman said, 'Okay,

80

that's good to know.' I asked the woman what the problem was, and she said she didn't think it was the appropriate time or place to discuss it. It was exactly the kind of middle-class response that had always baffled me.

While Cho was away on a course being run at Live Theatre in Newcastle, I met up with Ron for the first time in ages. I took him the *Paterson* DVD. As usual, when I got to Fuel, he was sat at his table in the corner.

He was running another of his poetry courses. This time it was the *Howl* workshop, where he talked about the Ginsberg poem and got people to write their own versions. There were two young women sat with him, and they listened attentively as Ron gave them the background to Ginsberg's poem and then played them bits from the three main sections of it, showing them how it was constructed.

Ron never charged people for his workshops. Money didn't matter to him and so he was shit with it, but I'd seen people charge eighty quid an hour for what he was giving away for free. And these two young women both shared what they had written, and it was pretty good for beginners, and they were amazed at themselves, they had never even read poems before, this was *literally* the first time, and Ron was greatly cheered, long after they'd left us to our drinking.

Rather than going on the beer, we'd decided to share a bottle of red wine between us for a change. It seemed like it could work out cheaper, but by early evening we were on to our third bottle.

'Hate this prose though, for the essays,' he said.

'Yeah, well you're almost at the end of your second year now.'

'I know. Flown by.'

'Yeah.'

'They've been good for me at Salford though. I'm so glad I didn't go to MMU. Much more friendly at Salford. At MMU when I applied it was like they didn't give a shit.'

'I remember you saying. They get loads there so they don't need to give a shit, do they?'

'No. Much more friendly at Salford though, all the tutors. But I'm looking forward to reading just what I want again.'

'Well you can do your dissertation next year.'

'Not decided what on yet.'

'Just do Ginsberg, or Creeley. Something to do with the Beats. That's your thing. You're already an expert so you'd be daft to do anything else. You could do a master's and then a PhD if you played your cards right.'

'My age you take it year by year,' he said, standing up.

I watched as he made his way upstairs to the toilet. I took the chance to give Cho a ring. We chatted for a bit about what she was doing in London, but she didn't like to talk about work.

'Are you drunk?' she asked.

'A bit.'

'Oh my god. How much have you had to drink?'

'About three bottles of wine.'

'Three bottles!'

'Not each.'

'Good, I should hope not. Is Ron drunk?'

'He's gone to the bog,' I said. 'He'll be ages yet.'

'Is he still skint?'

'He's always skint. He always will be.'

'Why doesn't he just get a job?' she said.

'Doing what?'

'Must be something he can do. It's called graft. I've never not worked.'

'I know but he's nearly sixty, got a bad knee. Spent all his years looking after his mum and dad.'

'Get a care job then.'

'But it's like he said, he doesn't want to wipe strangers' arses.'

'Eugh.'

'Exactly. That's the thing in this country. People say just get a job, but it isn't always that easy.'

'If you want to work you can work.'

'You sound like the Tories.'

'Well . . . '

Ron had spent twenty years looking after his mum and dad. He chose to do that, rather than putting them in a home, and it stopped him working anywhere else. Because of that he had no recent experience in anything. He'd started a degree not because of some pie in the sky bullshit, but because he could live on the loan payments for three years. And anyway, he was a fucking poet.

After he'd shuffled back down the stairs he started telling me about his old drinking days again.

'We were sitting in The Silver Birch and this bloke came in and he said where's your telly? Where's your telly, lads? We pointed up at the telly high in the corner and he walked over and unscrewed it from the wall and took it out. Later, when the landlord, Jimmy came downstairs to put on the football he said, where's the telly? And we said the bloke had come in and took it away. And Jimmy said, so you just let him take it? And it was like, well, he looked like that was what he was supposed to be doing. Good luck to him, that's what I said. Too much telly in pubs these days, there's matches every day. Better in here when it's just the banter. But Jimmy was up the wall. I'm surprised he noticed, the scan-eyed old twat. He's dead now. God bless.'

We drank more wine, and Ron talked about his dad again. 'He'd always say let's go down the lanes. And we did. The airport was still there but it was just tiny. One time we went to this motorway bridge and he told me to stop talking, because even then, you know I liked to talk, and so he told me to not talk for twenty minutes if I could, and we stood there on the motorway bridge, and eventually, like magic, a kestrel appeared, and it was hovering there, and because we were on the bridge we were at the same height, and I could see, even without the binoculars, how it's wings were flapping but it's head was totally still, and you could see the gleam in its eyes, and when dad came off the bridge he had a gleam in his eyes too. Other times he'd be looking at birds through his binoculars and I had a pencil and notepad and he would say the descriptions of the birds, like *dark stripe across the face* if it was a nuthatch or something and I'd have to write this stuff down. Even after his heart attack and when he needed the stick to walk he had the energy to go down 'the lanes' as he always called it. Ask anyone in Wythenshawe about the lanes and they'll know what you mean, older ones anyway.'

Late on, Ron came back from the bar with this old bloke in tow. 'This old reprobate here used to be my teacher,' he said.

'Oh thanks, Ron,' said the wiry old bloke. He had a London accent, sounded a bit rough. 'Been in The Vic, just popped in here for one.'

'He's my old adult education teacher,' said Ron, looking at me, 'when we could keep him out of the pub.'

'Those were the days. He had a lot of potential.'

'Yeah, whatever happened to that?' joked Ron.

'We all had potential at one time, Ron. I remember though, you were always writing stuff.'

'He's a poet now,' I said.

'*Poetry?* Fuck me. Would never have seen that one coming. Explains the red wine though. You still drink round near the college? I bumped into a few of my old colleagues from All Saints days and we're thinking of meeting up. What was it we used to go in, The Church, then the Sally, The Salutation? What's the Sally like these days?'

'Oh, not what it was. The uni took it over. Just not the same. You remember the cherry trees?' asked Ron.

'Yes, yes, I do, and do you know something, I went in there at ten o'clock one morning, you could do that then, I was in there at ten and it was filled with the workers who'd been in the night to chop the trees down. They were having a drink.'

'Oh yeah,' said Ron. 'There were massive complaints about it, a petition and everything, so they came in the night and fucking chopped them all down. Nobody knows what it used to be like out there. You could come out of the college as it was then and sit on the grass under the cherry trees.'

'Yes. No word of a lie,' said Chris, 'I was in the Sally the morning after. They'd just chopped them down and they were in there having a beer. Didn't blame them, of course, just doing their job.'

'Is the Vic your local now then?' asked Ron.

'Not really, still prefer The Friendship. That's still the best boozer round here. Got the best beer.'

'Did you ever go in Tommy Duck's?' I asked them.

'Oh yeah,' said Chris. 'You know something, the first time I ever went in there I thought what a great place this is, and I thought, I'll come in here again. Funny thing was, the very next day they closed it down.'

'You're a jinx,' said Ron.

'I know,' he said, laughing.

'Was that the place with the knickers on the ceiling?' I asked.

'Everyone says that,' said Ron.

'Yeah, we are better than that,' said Chris. 'There was more to that pub. It was huge.'

'Shame about the old pubs,' I said. 'I was looking online. There's pictures of some of them. Used to be loads down Oxford Road.'

'Oh yeah,' said Chris. 'You could go on a great pub crawl down there. You remember The Whitworth? That was a lovely pub, closed not that long ago. Some fucking social media café now.'

'Okay in here though?' I said.

'Oh yeah. Anyway, I was supposed to be back for ten. I can probably have one more. You're okay, aren't you? I'll get myself one in.'

'He really likes his ale,' said Ron. 'I think he had problems with it in the past.'

'Seems a nice bloke,' I said.

He came back and carried on chatting. 'You remember that bloke called Magic Steve?' said Chris.

'Yeah,' said Ron. 'Where was that?'

'I forget what pub it was. But he was a fucking fire-eater. You'd be standing at the bar and this big fucking flame would come shooting past you. It wasn't like it was a fucking act or anything!'

'I know, that was unreal. Anyway, what about your team these days, the happy Hammers?'

'Oh, don't ask. Your mob doing okay though? You were City, right?'

'Yeah, mate, happy days. Everyone hates us now. When we were shit everyone loved us. Now they hate us.'

'Well everyone still loves West Ham because we are shit,' he said, smiling. 'The youth system isn't there any more, the Lampard's, the Cole's, the Ferdinand's. The two Ferdinand lads. Not there now. Dirty Dicks, he was another fucking legend. Not the same these days. There's no investment and that new fucking ground's a disgrace, no fucking atmosphere I've been told, of course I don't get down there much these days.'

'You've got Zabaleta though?' said Ron.

'Yeah, but his fucking legs have gone.'

'Comes to us all,' said Ron. 'Bobby Moore, he was the one.'

'Ha, yeah, too true. He never had any legs in the first place! At least they've got a fucking statue now. Anyway lads, was great to meet you, I better get home.'

'Nice bloke,' I said, after he left.

'Oh yeah. Not many like him round now,' said Ron. 'Anyway, I think I'll be heading off as well.'

'Yeah.'

I left him at the bus stop where he waited for the 43. I carried on to Mauldeth Road and waited for the 25.

We stood on the crowded platform at Heaton Chapel, among the throngs of merry consumers, free from the shackles of work, heading into town to buy stuff we didn't really need. There was standing room only on the Northern Rail rattler from Buxton, bringing all the people from the countryside into central Manchester where they could do a bit of shopping, have a few beers and a bit of banter.

We got off the train and walked the back way out of Piccadilly, missing all the crowds and cutting down Dale Street. We carried on past Affleck's Palace and then went into the Arndale, past a greasy spoon café with paintings of old Coronation Street characters on the walls.

I wanted a watch and Cho wanted a big Stitch toy, from the cartoon *Lilo and Stitch*. It was kind of an adoption story, and I was sure I'd seen a little tear in Cho's eye by the end, though she denied it. It was *Kung Fu Panda* that really cut her up, the story of Po and Master Shifu and all them. There were hints at the adoption story in the first films but by *Kung Fu Panda* 3 it was all about Po discovering his birth father. I picked up a lovely silver watch from H Samuel, and Cho got a big fluffy Stitch from the Disney Store. Then she said she wanted a ring.

'I thought you didn't want a ring,' I said. 'The diamond mines and all that. Unethical.'

'I know but follow me.'

We went into Claire's, and Cho looked at some cheap metal rings, three for four quid, three for seven quid. Eventually she chose the seven quid ones and when I went to pay she snapped a photo of me with her phone.

Outside the shop I took one of the rings from the bag. Then I went down on my good knee.

'Will you marry me?' I asked, holding out the ring.

'What are you doing?'

'Will you marry me?'

'Yes. Now get up of the floor,' she said.

I put the ring on her finger and we made our way to the Waterstone's. They didn't stock any of my books, but you could get a decent cup of tea in the cafe. After that we went to Nando's.

On the crowded train back, there was a woman of about sixty, wearing sunglasses and leather pants, going on to another rock n' roll pensioner about getting home to her three-legged cat. He laughed at her and then blew up an inflatable Spiderman, which she then pretended to shag.

Back in The Vic with Ron, I got the Guinness in and we found a seat. There were tellies in all corners of the pub. If City won the game they'd win the league, and when we went two nil up at half time things were looking good. We should have been about five up.

'Worries me this,' said Ron. 'Mourinho's strategy is to play the second half. He sees where the team is at half time and then he takes it from there. Now they are two down they are going to have to come out and attack.'

'And Pep will keep attacking.'

'Exactly right, and Mourinho knows that.'

City should have gone three up when Gundogan hit the bar, but then it came, three United goals.

We sat there, silenced, the euphoria of the first half disappearing as quickly as our pints of Guinness. City should have had a penalty when Agüero was axed down by Ashley Young, and then De Gea pulled off a wonder save to keep out an Agüero header, and when Sterling missed yet another chance, hitting the post when it seemed easier to score, it was clear it wasn't going to be City's day.

At the roar of the reds at the final whistle, we necked our Guinness and headed back to Fuel, where the punters were more interested in falafel than football. We sat at Ron's usual round table in the corner. With no Guinness on tap, we made do with bottles of Stoodley Stout.

'What did I tell you about Mourinho?' said Ron.

'I don't want to talk about it.'

'I saw it coming, you could see it coming after we missed all those chances.'

'Not now, chief. But give me half an hour and I will be fine.'

'It's still all good, amigo.'

'Oh, I know.'

'Not like it was back in the day. You know, I've only ever wrote two letters to City. One to Tony Book, the great Tony Book, Skip they called him, and he wrote back, saying how thankful he was for my letter and how much he enjoyed hearing from fans. And then I wrote one to Alan Ball, when he was manager, years later. And Ball's letter came back, *thanks for your letter, but there's a reason I'm the manager and you are not. Don't forget I won the World Cup in 1966. What have you won?* And there was just a stamp at the bottom. Tony Book had signed his.'

'Ball was fucking clueless,' I said.

'I know. My letter was trying to give him some tactical awareness!'

'That's funny about the world cup. People said that about him, didn't they?'

'Yeah. He did fuck all after that. Nothing as a manager. And they were so shit in those days. I even stopped going for a while, I'm ashamed to say. But it was getting me down. That's what we must remember. For me more so than you, because I'm older, but I remember how depressed it used to make me, so I know how all those fans of other teams feel now, you even have to feel a bit sorry for Leeds . . . no scratch that, fuck Leeds, but there are these other teams, and it must be so grim to go and watch them. Someone like Sunderland, just gone to shit. And all that fan base. Aston Villa and Stoke. Stoke City. Imagine having to watch that shite week after week.'

'I know. But watching anyone is shite compared to watching City. Even United. Pep plays the beautiful game. I'd have loved to play in that side. Just keep passing it around. Beautiful stuff.'

'Enjoy it, amigo. I am. It was shit for a long time and now it's all good. It won't last forever.'

'Hey, on an even lighter note, did you see they got that Bennell?'

'Ha. Tell me about it.'

'Was he there when you were?'

'No, but Broome was. They mentioned him.'

'Oh right.'

'Broome was there when I played for Whitehill. We trained in Cheadle, near the river there. Hardly touched the ball. Did all this running, throwing medicine balls at each other. We wore cast off kits from the youth team, sometimes the reserves. If it was a reserves one it would drown you, you'd have to roll the sleeves right up and that.'

'So, this Broome coached you, did he?'

'Yeah.'

'And he's another Bennell?'

'Well he's dead now, but yeah, he was mentioned in the report.'

'Fucking hell, there but for the grace of god and all that.'

'Well, yeah. Makes you think back. Like why did he tell us to take our underpants off before we put our shorts on? When you're a kid you don't think. It sounds daft, but I thought it was something technical.'

'That sounds well dodgy.'

'Oh, I know, but in those days, you didn't even think about it. And why was he always walking around in the changing room?'

'Fuck's sake.'

'I think I was okay because my Mum and Dad were there every game. And then I got injured. My Dad carried me off, and they just put ice on it and that was it. Great fucking physio that isn't it? And after that I couldn't be arsed going back.'

'Right.'

'To be honest I hated all that running around, the medicine balls and all that. It was too knackering. Anyway, are you going back to the bar?'

'Course. Same as?'

'Yeah.'

'We still on for Wednesday?' he said, when I got back with the pints.

'Oh yes. I'm not sure the book will have arrived, but if it hasn't I will just read some off my phone, give it a plug anyway.'

'Sounds good. It was a bit shit last time. Literally three of us there. And Johnny had brought his guitar.'

'Did he play?'

'There was no point. There were three of us. I tell you, I'm thinking of giving it up. Not the magazine, but the night.'

'Why? Some nights it's full up. You never know.'

'I know, but there's only so many times you can big it up to people. And if you big it up to them, and then they come and there's nobody here, they don't come back.'

'Yeah but people are stupid like that. They think because there's lots of people there it must be good. And if there aren't then it can't be. In my experience it's often quite the opposite. But people follow the crowd.'

'There's been a bit of a change, I think. Everything must be in the centre of town these days. And it is different with the magazine too. I think poets just want to perform now, get a show, read something out on a fucking advert for Nationwide Insurance. They aren't interested in publication. We aren't getting any submissions in for the magazine.'

'That's a shame. It's people like you give new writers an outlet. It's how I started.'

'Will just see how it goes.'

'Thing is, Ron, we are playing the long game. Put together a body of work and people will start to take notice. They'll see.'

'I wish I could be as sure about that as you. What if it isn't true?'

'I'm happy with my books. I know they're pretty good. And I know I keep improving.'

'What if nobody ever notices?'

'Look, I don't really give a fuck. I just keep doing my own thing, follow my instincts, not the crowd.'

'That's what I mean about the poetry. Everybody wants a fucking show. It's bollocks. None of that work will last.'

'You're right. Depends what you want out of it I guess.

There's that argument that you're not writing for posterity. But maybe you should.'

'I'm not sure things are like that anymore. But the good thing is that I have the magazine. And it isn't based in London and isn't part of the establishment. And that's what we need more of.'

'Outsiders, chief. That's what we are.'

'Are you going to the bar?'

'Yeah. Same again?'

'Yes.'

It was the usual barman, tall bloke with an artist's beard and a beret. A lovely bloke, kind to drunks. Ron said he'd been named after Colin Bell.

'You know the best thing about Alan Ball,' said Ron when I got back. 'The best thing was that song. You remember? *And after all, you're my Alan Ball*'?

'Oh yeah. Oasis.'

'Still a shit manager though.'

Just then, Ruff wandered in. He had grey dreadlocks and had run a young writer's group in Manchester for years. 'You okay?' he asked, smiling.

'Alright mate,' I said. 'Long time no see.'

'Yeah, was the fundraiser I think.'

'Yeah, I remember you saying what a great night you had. How's it going Ron?'

'Not bad, amigo. When you going to find me the new Baraka?'

'Ha ha.'

'What's he on about?' I asked.

'It's because I'm black, right Ron?'

'Ha, ha, yeah that's why.'

'I was telling Ron, last time I was in. About Baraka. Amira Baraka. We both saw him read in Manchester, at the uni. But I was saying about him, when he got banned in America for his nine eleven poem. I was in Jamaica, saw him at Calabash. And he was this little old man, frail, he could barely make it out onto the stage, but when he started reading his poem he set the stage on fire, it was incredible!'

'You know I published him?' said Ron. 'Tried to get him to read for us. But his agent was a tosser. Well maybe not a tosser, but very protective. Wanted money just for talking to him.'

'I've not read him,' I said.

'Best reading I've ever seen,' said Ruff.

'The Fuel stage awaits the new generation!' said Ron, even though he was stopping the night.

'I'll drink to that!' said Ruff, and we stayed in there all night, still drinking as Colin stacked chairs on the other tables.

It used to look a right shithole when you came out of Stockport train station, but they had tarted it up in recent years, with a Holiday Inn, a Sainsbury's, a big car park and a new, sweeping front, where the road curved around the corner and past the McDonald's to Wellington Road. We headed the other way, around the side of the Sainsbury's towards the town hall.

We ticked our names off at reception and then walked into the hall, where all kinds of stalls were set up. We were given a goodie bag and then offered some bucks fizz, which I gladly sipped. We started to wander around. There were photographers, florists, car hire places, cake makers, suit hire. We tried two cake makers, one gave us a tiny sample, the other a big box of cake, and Cho smiled as we tucked into it. All the while there was this atrocious music going on, a kind of comatose saxophone.

We sat down for a bit to eat more cake and decided that the small sample had been the tastiest. She was a nice woman from Hazel Grove and had said we could arrange to visit her nearer the time for a tasting session.

The saxophone duo paused briefly, and we looked over as a snowy haired DJ in a bow tie whispered into his microphone, 'Lovely tunes from Note Perfect there. Great work, gentlemen, keep it going. Can we have a round of applause for Note Perfect?'

There was a smattering of hand claps, and we joined in, before the DJ continued, 'Just to let you know, the lovely ladies in our fashion show will be coming on again at two o'clock, that's two o'clock for the lovely young ladies. Some beautiful dresses on show, that's two o'clock, ladies and gentlemen.'

The saxophone duo started up again. 'Baker Street', followed by some Curtis Stigers.

'This music is awful,' said Cho.

'They are doing their best, I suppose.'

'I think if we had music like that at our wedding I would kill myself.'

'What are we going to do until two?'

'What do *you* want to do?'

'I'd rather go home.'

'No, I want to see this fashion show.'

'Well, let's go and get something to eat.'

'Okay.'

We headed back out onto Wellington Road. It was still snowing a bit and we couldn't be arsed walked into town to the Mersey Way Shopping Centre for the usual option of Gregg's or Halshaw's or the Pound Bakery, and just went to the Sainsbury's near the train station. I got a sandwich and Cho got a bag of Doritos. The sun shone in through the windows, and there was hardly anyone in the shop, so we sat on a couple of empty chairs by the self-service checkout.

'Oh, the romance,' said Cho.

'Not bad in here,' I said.

When Cho had nearly finished the big bag of Doritos, she passed me what was left and took her big water bottle out of her bag and drank. Then she opened the goodie bag and seemed pleased with the free magazines, *Cheshire Bride* and *County Brides*. She'd done some modelling and loved glossy magazines to flick through, checking out the poses of the models as well as the clothes. There were lots of flyers in the bag as well, and some Love Hearts that she gave me because she said they were disgusting.

We headed back to the town hall and took our seats on the front row, listening as the saxophone duo ploughed on. It was with some sense of relief all round that they finished. I gave them a clap but Cho didn't bother.

The snowy haired DJ introduced the fashion show and I looked around. There were a lot of bottle blonde women there, with younger bottle blonde women who I presumed to be their daughters. And there were clearly a few couples in love. But among them was a sad looking woman who seemed to be on her own.

There were two models that showed off the wedding dresses, and they looked happy as they walked carefully down the cat walk. But the models for the bridesmaid's dresses were all teenage girls and they looked terrified as they walked gingerly along the cat walk in their high heels, clearly thinking that they might trip themselves up at any moment. At the end they all looked mightily relieved, smiling over at their parents in the audience.

Cho took one or two pictures of dresses she liked during the show, but she already knew she'd be wearing a traditional Chinese Cheongsam dress for the wedding, so I didn't get the point of it. But there had been cake and she seemed happy. When I looked at my phone I saw that City were winning, and realized I'd be able to catch the second half when we got home.

I got into the staff room at Tameside and Andrea was there, eating a cake. Andrew was pretending to do something on the computer and ignoring everyone around, Katherine had gone out for a fag, and Paul was adjusting one of his hearing aids. Then Barbara came bustling in.

'Oh, my lord, that traffic is disgusting. And you can't predict it, that's the problem. I set off at the same time yesterday and I was fifteen minutes early. I'm sorry Andrew but it's just one of those things.'

Andrew nodded. I watched as Barbara unloaded a load of sugary snacks onto the table. I'd worked with someone like that in my old library job. They liked to feed people.

Katherine came in. 'I see that fucking dumbo in the office is back,' she said. 'What's her name? Fucking hell. We get them all here.'

She saw me smirking, and it seemed to encourage her. I noticed that she never wore her lanyard.

'This college is a fucking shambles. The management are a joke. I'm sorry Andrew, but it needs to be said.'

Andrew kept his head firmly pointed towards the computer.

He appeared to have been writing the same email for about half an hour. Then he got up.

'Right folks, I'm off. See you later,' he said.

'Short and sweet,' said Andrea, as the door closed.

'Does fuck all,' said Katherine. 'Spends most of his time in his car. Marching not fighting, that's what they call that.'

'What do you mean?' asked Andrea.

'Well, when he's driving he's not working is he? I'd put a fucking tracker on that car of his.'

'I think you are harsh,' said Barbara.

'Fuck off,' said Katherine.

'No, I really do. And I've told you, I don't know why you need to swear so much.'

'Who you with today, Barbara?' asked Katherine.

'New lad. Elliot.'

'Oh right.'

'Yeah. He's got no arms.'

'What course is he on?'

'Sports Science.'

'Sports Science?'

'Yeah. Basketball this morning.'

Katherine smirked at me, then at Andrea, before laughing out loud. Andrea restrained herself, her face red.

'What's so funny?' said Barbara.

'I'm sorry, but, how the fuck is he going to play basketball when he doesn't have any arms?'

'I can't believe you are taking that attitude.'

'Well, come on.'

'My attitude is 'there for the grace of god go I'. You shouldn't be making fun of it,' said Barbara, picking up her handbag and leaving the staffroom.

'Seems upset,' I said.

'Oh, she'll fucking get over it. Barbara fucking Windsor, comes tottering in in those high heels. She's never in the fucking classroom. She's never on time. You've got to have a laugh in this fucking job. On these wages. She thinks she's all that, yet she does fuck all. You go out there and watch. That poor bastard will be trying to play basketball and then she fucking turns up with her high heels and painted fucking nails, what's the point?'

'See what you mean.'

'Anyway, Billy no mates, who are you with today?'

'Was supposed to be with Iffy. But he's off.'

'Has he pissed himself yet?'

'Not that I know of.'

'Oh Katherine, you are awful,' said Andrea.

'I know. I'm going for another fag before nine. See you later.'

'She's only having a laugh,' said Andrea, after Katherine had left. 'The students love her. She's been here for years. Talk about an advocate. She stands up for her students. Not like most of them here.'

'Oh, I know,' I said. 'I can tell that.'

'You know she'll have had to leave her house at about half seven this morning to go and bring Molly in on the bus. And she'll walk her to the bus stop later, makes sure she gets on. And half the time she's not getting paid for any of that. She's knows more than any of these managers. And she's been offered it, management, but she told them where to go. So anyway, oh shit, look at the time, I've got to go. See you later.'

I sat in the silent staff room, looking at the two clocks side by side together on the wall. One said five past nine, the other five past eight. There had been some argument with management about who changed the clocks when they needed to go forward or back, and the outcome had been that they had one clock for summer, one for winter. I looked out through the window, down into the courtyard to the animal care department. They had Japanese raccoon dogs down there. Katherine said they'd got a job lot of them in some dodgy deal.

Wandering around the room, I looked in boxes stacked on desks. I got a packet of black biro pens, a small notebook and a blue marker pen, and put them in my coat pocket. I was supposed to stay until at least lunch time. I had my sandwiches and banana and sat looking out of the window at the hills above Stalybridge, the two clocks ticking on the wall.

There was a time they used to call Stalybridge 'Staly Vegas' and it was only half joking in those days because the pubs and bars around the centre of town used to be rocking. But when I had a wander round at lunchtime there seemed to be only about two pubs still going, and the wind whistled off the hills and through a ghost town.

I was with Ron again in Fuel, when Bill popped his head in. He was carrying a bag of washing. He brought it in and put it under the desk and we got a bottle of red wine and three glasses. I'd not seen Bill for a while, since we'd helped Ron in tidying up his house. He still had the right stem of his glasses taped on, and he still wore the shoes that Ron had given him during the clear up. He'd been volunteering at the jazz festival for years, and both his rucksack and t-shirt were freebies from that. I'm not sure he ever actually bought any clothes.

I'd first seen Bill in Bury, years before when he was a boring poet, his hesitant stumbling voice wading through stuff he didn't even really like himself. But he discovered the William Burroughs cut-up method and when he got red wine in him his eyes glinted. He was a poet to his boots, even more so than Ron in the sense that you thought Ron could probably do other things, but for Bill it was poetry, all or nothing.

He wrote a poem and then folded the page and cut it into pieces, before re-arranging those pieces to get unusual and interesting sentences that took the poems to places they wouldn't have otherwise gone to. When people heard them at Fuel they were puzzled, but they engaged with his open, drunken style of delivery that showed he wasn't too uptight about the whole thing.

Several other poets I knew kept popping up on TV ads for Nationwide Insurance. Ron used to get well pissed off about it. I wonder how much they got paid, and whether that was worth what they lost from their soul? At least Gary Mike's was a good poem. I looked on Twitter. But you could see right through some of the others. Someone had a picture of himself donating blood, another showed a cat she'd rescued, another was asking for money for her charity run up Kilimanjaro. How could you not read their books? Such wonderful humanitarians.

I'd have bitten your hand off for a couple of hundred quid to read something on an advert though. Bill and Ron would have been great on it too and always needed the money. Who can afford scruples under a government that would rather you die than claim benefit?

This was around the time they were making the Windrush generation apply for passports when it was us wanted them here to do our shitty jobs in the first place. The brazen blanket hypocrisy and sheer cruelty of the Tory government was beginning to sicken me on a daily basis, and I could no longer watch BBC news channels because once the seed was sowed in my mind that they were biased in favour of the government, I saw chinks of that bias in every sentence, every gesture, in every frown on every face and in every line of questioning.

'You know about Robert Donat, don't you?' said Bill, sipping his red wine.

'Name rings a bell.'

'*The Thirty-Nine Steps* was his most famous one. He used to drink round here. They called it the Three Lions. You've got the Red Lion still going, but the White Lion has gone, it's the Sainsbury's now, and then there was the Golden Lion near Christie's. And Donat used to get drunk in all of them. He was born here, in Withington I think. There's a plaque somewhere.'

'*Goodbye, Mr Chips?*' said Ron.

'That's right,' said Bill. 'That was another one of his.'

After finishing his wine, Bill took his laundry home, said he'd be back later. It was the poetry night that Ron said he was going to stop doing, he was always saying that, and always brought it back after a few months off. I read some new flash fictions, Ron practiced a couple of his old poems and then it was Bill's turn. He had a big pile of paper in his hands. It was a pile that grew with every new poem he wrote. He read a poem and then threw it to the floor. He carried on in a red wine whirlwind, reeling one magical poem off after another, interspersed with the occasional bout of coughing. At the end he went down on his knees and picked the poems up off the floor.

As he picked up his poems we could hear a banging up the stairs. It was Harry Fagan, the one-legged poet from

Skelmersdale. He'd lost his leg in the Falklands and had been writing poems about his disability ever since. He'd even had a show on at the Contact, another at the Royal Exchange.

'Alright to go right on, Ron?'

'Yeah, go for it mate.'

'Alright you cunts, you might have noticed my disability here? That's right, I'm deaf in one ear. No really, I've got some new ones, I wrote some of these today. Can't read my own handwriting.'

It took him a while to warm up, but his poems were great. Honest, no hiding behind intellect or technique. And after he read he just went home. Shortly after that Hannah Mercy turned up, one of the few female poets to appear on the Fuel stage. It was always great to hear that female perspective, but she also had a voice all her own, and she read her poems about the misogyny she experienced while riding her bike around Manchester.

The two late additions had made it a great night, and the four of us left kept drinking until well after twelve when Colin started putting the chairs on the tables. Hannah got on her bike and wobbled off down Wilmslow Road, me and Ron got our buses, and Bill walked back to his flat on Mauldeth Road.

Cho never came to Fuel. She said it was full of middle-aged white men and the toilets were disgusting. I couldn't argue with that, and anyway she was cool with us doing our own thing. She just stayed at home and, when she wasn't working on the laptop, watched awful TV like *Keeping Up with the Kardashians*, *Extreme Cake Makers*, *Millionaire Match Maker*, *Dance Moms* or *The Bachelor*. *The Bachelor* was about the only one of those I could stand, but there were one or two other programmes we watched together. *University Challenge* was one, and for the first few rounds we did okay. We kept score and usually got about ten questions right each, but when the series reached the semi finals and the final the questions just got silly. By then we were just guessing which of the contestants were virgins.

I met up with Scoie in the Piccadilly Tap, a newish place on the approach to the train station. Glass fronted, with a bar in the middle and wood panelling on all the walls, I didn't like it at first. There was a chalkboard with all the ales written on it, and after a couple called Holy Ghost, I started feeling better and the bar began to remind me of a bar in the Bukowski film, *Factotum*. There a scene in that where he's watching a pole dancer on the bar, and he's going on about being a writer, and he says, 'if you are going to go, go all the way.'

It was mid-afternoon, swarming hordes going up and down the hill outside. Light shone in across the tables, and across the floor, as a handful of men, including me and Scoie, sat around sipping our pints. I recognized the barmaid's face, from years before, but I didn't know where. She said she'd worked in the Marble Arch on Rochdale Road, but I couldn't remember ever having gone in there.

'Got some jokes for you,' said Scoie. 'Now on sale at IKEA - beds for lesbians: no nuts or screwing involved, it's all tongue and groove.'

'Very good.'

'A Muslim has been shot with a starting pistol; police say it's definitely race related.'

'Mmm . . .'

'Due to a water shortage in Ireland, Dublin swimming baths have announced they are closing lanes seven and eight.'

'Irish jokes, *right*.'

'I got a letter from Screw Fix Direct thanking me for my interest, but explaining they were not a dating agency.'

'No wonder the suffragette movement got started.'

'The lead actor in the local pantomime production of Aladdin was shagged by the gay genie on stage last night – to be fair the audience did try to warn him.'

'Genius.'

'Such an unfair world. When a man talks dirty to a woman it's considered sexual harassment. When a woman talks dirty to a man it's two quid a minute.'

'Another one for Emily Pankhurst.'

'Got stopped in the street outside Boots today by a woman with a clipboard asking, "What products do I use for grooming?" She was a bit taken aback when I replied, "Facebook".'

'Dodgy.'

'Just booked a table for Valentine's Day for me and the wife. Bound to end in tears though – she's crap at snooker.'

'Are we in the 1970's?'

'Got a new Jack Russell pup today, he's mainly black and brown with just a small white area so I've called him Bradford.'

'Yep. I think you've covered everything now.'

'If you get an email telling you that you can catch Swine Flu from tins of ham then delete it. It's Spam.'

'That's not bad. You see that's fine.'

'They say that sex is the best form of exercise. Now correct me if I'm wrong but I don't think two minutes every six months is going to shift this beer belly.'

'Speak for yourself.'

'When I was a kid people used to cover me in chocolate

and cream and put a cherry on my head. Yeah, life was tough in the gateau.'

'Now that's funny. Yeah, I guess that's okay. Not sure about the others though.'

'Come on, you were dying to laugh.'

'I really wasn't, chief.'

At least there were no Chinese jokes. He'd tried one once and I told him he was well out of order. We had a few more beers and I waved him off as he headed for his tram back to Droylsden, but I was just getting in the mood and a seat at the bar was too hard to resist. I got myself another pint and watched the place fill up with the after-work crowd.

I got more and more hemmed in at the bar and had drink after drink to try and feel relaxed, but I hated crowds. I walked down to The Waterhouse near the library. Had a cheap pint and a meal. Even in there it was too busy. I went upstairs to the toilet and a bloke had pissed on the floor.

In the old drinking days, I'd have gone on a wander, probably cutting down Dale Street to sit at the bar in Night and Day, another American looking place where I could pretend to be Bukowski. Where else? Mulligan's, maybe, round the back of Deansgate. But that wasn't the same as it had been. All big screens and lager. There were no quiet places in central Manchester anymore, it was just people everywhere. No end to the frenzy. I got on a tram outside the library and stood there with a bloke's armpit in my face.

Back in Heaton Moor I went to The Elizabethan. A lovely old pub but like the Moor Top at the other end of the road, just set up for meals. All menus and kids and large, sparkly wine glasses. Twelve-year old's in aprons pretending to be bar staff. I wandered down to The Plough, and it was the same kind of thing. All too clean, somehow, too family friendly. The Crown was better. The best kind of pub, the kind you can't see into from outside. Filled with regulars. Barmaids who like to drink on the job. I went in the public bar and got myself a Guinness. Looking across into the tap room I saw one of my neighbours from the flats. An old guy, he sat on a barstool staring at the wall.

Every time Cho got off the train I'd go and meet her, but on this night, I messaged her to say I was in The Crown and said for her to pop in on the way back. There was no reply, but what seemed soon after, she appeared in the doorway, frowned at me, then turned around and went back out. I gulped down the last of my pint and caught up with her.

'God, you looked so sad in there,' she said.

'I don't feel sad.'

'You looked like a loser. A saddo.'

'Well you weren't at home, so I stayed out.'

'You've got drunk face,' she said.

'Well I've been out since one this afternoon.'

'Where's Scoie? Why are you drinking on your own?'

'He never stays out any more.'

When we got back she went for a wee. I followed her into the bathroom.

'You are so naughty,' she said, as I gargled mouthwash.

'I'll have a shower in a bit,' I said.

'Don't care, drunk face.'

At the end of the college term I got some more agency work, this time in a call centre at a business park called The Flowers. I went on my bike and locked it up in the underground car park. After giving my name in at reception I was given a green lanyard with the name of the agency written on it, and a blank swipe card to open doors.

The training week was a laugh with characters like Bobo, Jibbin and Abdulla, three students doing the job to help pay for their studies. They were all over six feet tall and Abdulla was about twenty-five stone and got through enough bottled water to fill a swimming pool.

A camp Scottish lad did the training and it was the usual bullshit. They took us through every conceivable aspect of the job just on the off chance that someone called about that, but really it was just to cover their arses legally. But where the permanent staff had had five weeks training, we had a week.

Every now and again we were asked to stand in a circle and throw a little basketball to each other and say something we had learned about the company. Once you'd said something you sat down. One day there was a Lucozade promotion, so they handed out all these mini cans of Lucozade.

The canteen was good, decent food and cheap, but agency staff weren't allowed to sit in the Partner's Restaurant. All the permanent employees were called partners, and they were eligible for discounts at hotels and gyms and afternoon tea at Harvey Nick's or Patisserie Valerie. You could see all the offers on the walls of the canteen. There were also photos for employees of the month. They called them 'Roof Raisers'. We'd sit in there having lunch and the managers would walk past us and sit together in the Partner's Restaurant.

Some people got sacked during the training. One lad for coming in late twice, another for answering his phone while the training was going on. Connor, the lad from the agency, came along to see how we were all getting on with the training. He smiled, said he was there for us whenever we needed him, and then explained that there might have been some confusion but now it had been clarified that we wouldn't be getting paid for our breaks.

At the end of the training week they gave us our various shift patterns. Mine was Tuesday to Saturday, eight until half four one week, half eight until five the next week, and then nine until half five the week after that. Some of the others were doing twelve-hour shifts, four days on and three days off.

When we turned up to do live calls the first week I found myself sat near Bobo, Jibbin and Abdulla. The managers were Lisa, Sally and Wendy, three young women who nibbled on crisps and drank fizzy drinks all day. As I looked around the room nearly everyone was fat. There was also a dwarf in a tiara, a hunchback, and a bearded transvestite wearing cowboy boots and a pink Stetson. A few people in wheelchairs too. The kind of people they didn't want on the shop floor.

From where I sat I could see a screen high up in the corner. It showed the daily profits and then the weekly ones. One day it was £8,432,217. It was always something like that. Millions of pounds per day, per week, and yet the company was making massive losses. They seemed complacent. I couldn't see anything improving for them anytime soon. None of us sounded great on the phone, but Abdulla was the worst, he just shouted at people.

Bobo was a bright lad, the job too easy for him, and he was almost horizontal in his chair, even though they'd told us about the importance of posture. Jibbin was a funny lad. He had a scar on his cheek from some childhood incident in India after which they stitched him up badly, and he was a big lad, but the smiley face and the glasses made him look friendly. He was doing Sports Management at MMU. Half the time you didn't really know if he was on the phone because he was always messing around, saying things like, 'Oh hello, Cristiano Ronaldo, no, I'm afraid you can't buy the company, even if you bare rich blood,' or 'Jay Z, morning blood, you want three hundred pairs of trainers, okay blood, I will just sort that out for you now. How would you like to pay? American Express Gold Card. No problem. My name? Jibbin. Don't forget it. No problem, you have a good day now. Say hello to Beyoncé for me', or 'Jose Mourinho? How can I help? You want some respect? Okay let's see what we can do.'

Chris was an architecture student, doing an MA at Manchester Uni. Went on about sustainable housing, had lived in a wooden hut the previous summer as part of his dissertation. Wes wasn't a student, had worked in call centres the last few years, was savvy on the phones, showed me how logging on and off could help you avoid getting a call just before your break or the end of your shift. Don was an actor, bald, a bit bonkers and always wore shorts above hairy white legs. Ryan had a low boredom threshold, and always wanted to play quizzes and games between calls. Michelle was on the ball, well serious, travelled four hours per day on the buses and really needed the work. Sabha was quite bolshie, you could hear her arguing the toss at times with customers, and the managers didn't like her, and she was gone before the end of the first week. By then only twelve of us were left out of the thirty-odd that did the training. Mercedes got sacked after she came in smelling of booze, Menara lost her voice and they let her go as well.

On the day of the royal wedding between Prince Harry and Meghan Markle, a TV was set up in front of the managers desk, and people came in wearing union jack t-shirts, or dresses. Leo, the dwarf, had come in wearing the tiara, and every time he walked up and down in his role as floorwalker, the managers hugged him to their breasts or kissed the top of his bald head. He was just so adorable. Thankfully I couldn't see the TV from my desk. The phones were quiet as the wedding got underway. I sat there looking at the sales figures on the TV screen.

On my lunchbreak I wolfed down my food and then wandered to the cricket ground next door to sit in the sun. Then I called Cho and we chatted about the scripts she was reading for the National Theatre. Everyone was trying to write a dystopia after the success of *The Handmaid's Tale* on TV and they were all shit and full of men being horrible to women. I went back in to work. Outside the main entrance there were loads of workers sitting down on bean bags, looking at their phones. You weren't allowed to have your phone on you while working. You left it in the locker room, and when you went in there you could hear them all ringing and vibrating.

I sat back down at my desk, put the headphones on and waited for the beep. I answered.

'Good afternoon, how can I help?'

'Oh, yeah. I want a washing machine,' said the young woman. A baby was crying loudly in the background and she tried to quieten it down.

'Do you know the product code?'

'Erm . . . what's that?' she said, as the baby screamed.

'Product code . . . or you can just tell me the name of it?'

'Miele.'

'Okay,' I said, searching under the product names. 'Do you know the price?'

'Two thousand, hundred and forty-nine.'

'Okay, so that's the WKR 771 Twindos Quick Powerwash Freestanding washing machine?'

'That's it.'

'Okay can I just take your email address then please?'

She gave me an email address and then her home address. The baby continued to cry.

'Would you like five years added care on that, for one hundred and fifty pounds?'

'What's that?'

'You get added care on it. Anything goes wrong you get it repaired for free.'

'Okay, yes.'

'You also get six months of free detergent.'

'Erm . . . okay.'

I confirmed her delivery address and then asked for her payment details.

She gave me the number on the card, and then the three-digit security number at the back.

'I'm afraid the card hasn't been accepted,' I said.

The baby was still crying. The young woman hesitated, then hung up.

I looked over at Jibbin, who was twirling around on his chair.

'She was well dodgy,' I said.

'Why?'

'Just hung up when the card didn't go through.'

'Yeah, I've had that.'

I heard another beep in my ear. 'Good afternoon, how can I help?'

'Oh hello. After shave,' the man said.

'Right?'

'What do you know about it?'

'To be honest I've never worn it.'

'Oh dear. How do you get on with the ladies?'

'Erm . . . okay.'

'Yeah . . . I bet. Eau de parfum.'

'Okay.'

'What have you got?'

I typed it into the search bar, read out some of the brands. 'Okay so we've got Creed, Tom Ford, Hermes, Atelier.'

'What Tom Ford have you got?'

'Private Blend. White Suede, Tobacco Vanilla, Tuscan Leather, Oud Wood.'

'Oh yeah, how much have you got the Oud Wood on at?'

'Three eighty.'

'And that's the two fifty mil?'

'That's right.'

'Okay I will have that. And what Creed have you got?'

'Viking, Aventus, Green Irish Tweed, Royal Oud.'

'I'll have some of the Aventus. But in the fifty mil.'

'That's one seventy.'

'Okay that's fine.'

'Maybe I should try some myself.'

'Take it from me, son, I'm seventy years old.'

'Oh right.'

'Seventy is nothing these days, isn't that right love?'

I heard a woman laughing in the background.

'Okay then, so if I can just take your email?'

I took his details and he chose the Click and Collect option, picking up the next afternoon from the Bluewater branch.

After wrapping up the call I sat around for a bit. There

were a few more calls and then finally it was break time. I'd realized by now that it must have been impossible for the managers to check everyone's break times and how long we had, so I took off my headphones, walked to the door, pressed the green button and then went out, down the stairs and out through the front door.

There were only two bean bags left, and I sat in one of them for a bit. I looked up at the glass frontage of the call centre building, and then around at the tall trees. There were some jays high up in one of them, causing a racket with their grating calls. I got up and went for a wander around the business park. At the back there was a big old building with a blue plaque on for someone I'd never heard of, and a grassy area with picnic tables. A squirrel hurtled across the grass. I went and sat at one of the tables. Then I got up and lay on top of it, staring up at fading vapour trails. I could hear the sound of willow on leather, the shout of an LBW appeal, thought back to that fifty partnership with Del.

After a break of about thirty minutes I got up off the picnic table and walked back to the call centre, bent forward so the swipe card on my lanyard could reach the door and open it, went up the stairs and did the same again with the card to get through two more doors. Jibbin was still twirling around on his seat.

'You okay blood?' he said.

'Not bad.'

'They are checking the breaks you know,' he said with a smile.

'No worries,' I said, smiling back.

I put the headphones on and after a couple of minutes looking out of the window, the beep sounded in my ears.

'Oh hello,' she said. 'I've been faffing around on your bloody website for hours.'

'Sorry to hear that.'

'What?'

'I said I'm sorry to hear that.'

'You'll have to speak up, lad. I'm ninety.'

'Ninety, oh right.'

'Bathroom scales I'm after. What do you suggest?'

'Let's just have a look.'

'What?'

'There's the Terralion Digital Ultra Slim Glass Scale. Special buy at fourteen ninety-nine?'

'Glass?'

'Yeah, glass.'

'Don't want glass.'

'Okay, well, there's the flat digital scale at twenty pounds.'

'Digital did you say?'

'Yeah.'

'Not digital, I want a dial one, and one that I can see properly. I have trouble seeing the digital ones.'

'Okay, let's look. Okay, there's the Salter. Heston Blumenthal dual precision . . . oh hang on, that's for the kitchen.'

'Salter?'

'Yes, but that was a kitchen scale.'

'I don't need a kitchen scale, lad, it is a bathroom scale I want.'

'I know, I know. Okay so there's the Classic Mechanical Bathroom Scale. Thirty-five pounds.'

'What is the dial like? Will I be able to read the dial?'

'The digital ones are probably easier to read.'

'No digital, don't want digital.'

'Okay well there's that thirty-five pound one, and the academy one at seventy pounds.'

'Why is that one seventy pounds and the other thirty-five, what's the difference?'

'Well I will have a look at the details. Okay so this one has a bigger dial on it. Also has a non-slip platform for up to size twelve feet?'

'Size twelve?'

'Non-slip.'

'Oh well, I'm in a dilemma now, I don't know which one to choose. What do you think?'

'Well the seventy pound one is more expensive, but the dial is better. Bigger, easier for you to see. And it has a fifteen-year guarantee.'

'What?'

'It has got a fifteen-year guarantee on it.'

'Ha ha ha! Fifteen years!'

'Shall we go for that one then?'

'You think I'm going to live another fifteen years, lad? Okay let's go for that one then.'

'Okay. You can always return it.'

'Oh yes, I can can't I. Okay then.'

'Great. Can I get your email address then please?'

'Oh, I don't bugger around with all that.'

'Postal address?'

She gave me her details and we proceeded to payment. I asked her for the number on her bank card.

'Oh . . . something seven, I think, oh hang on, I'll just go for the magnifying glass.'

I could hear her shuffling around and cursing in the

background. When she came back she read me the numbers and the payment went through.

'Okay love, thank you,' she said.

'My pleasure.'

'Thank you, you have been a great help to me.'

'That's fine.'

'No, I'm really grateful, thank you for your help.'

'Okay.'

'Bye then.'

'Bye.'

The rest of the shift was quiet, and when it was over I went downstairs to the changing room. I opened my little locker and took out my phone and keys, phones vibrating or ringing in lockers all around me, then walked over to the underground car park where my bike was locked up. I cycled out to the traffic lights, went straight ahead, past the Didsbury Hotel on my left and then cut through onto Parrswood Road, making my way home past the big Tesco in Burnage.

Waiting in the cool early morning on Heaton Moor Road, the car, the only one on the road, turned up and it was Shackie and Scoie, big Shackie driving and Scoie in front. I chucked my rucksack in the boot with theirs and we hit the road, me lying down in the back.

I looked up now and again to see fleeting trees and then finally got up to see the Howgill fells, glorious from the M6, and soon we came off there after the services, where we sat in our shades and drank coffee. Then we were on the A roads in the Scottish sun, A78, A71, and on through Saturday morning scenes: a dazzling pair of young women dolled up and laughing, on their way home after the night before, old boys tapping rolled up newspapers on their pale white legs, village stores, little yapping dogs on leads, brief glimpses of footpaths, bits of the Southern Upland Way, and it was one curving stretch after another as Shackie leaned into the wheel and we listened to old tunes for old time's sake, the swirling keyboards of the Inspiral Carpets, a bit of The Stone Roses. Eventually I could see over towards the coast and Troon and the distant peaks of Arran I knew so well, but it was only before we passed Charlie's Bar on our way through the streets of Ardrossan with its bowling hall and newsagents and churches that we came into town with a view across the water of magical Arran. We waited awhile to get the car aboard the ferry and then we did and got out and climbed the steep stairs and joined the line for food, all three of us getting a big plate of fish and chips. By the time that was eaten it was time to head out on deck and walk around into the wind at the front of the boat, holding our caps and taking pictures with the glorious sight of Arran behind us, all those peaks I'd rambled across on previous visits. Soon enough it was time to get off the ferry and we drove up and over the hill into Lamlash, down past the golf course, the view of Holy Island opening up, that big rock plonked in the bay and home to Buddhists, and we turned right and drove through Lamlash, past the café and The Drift Inn and The Pierhead Tavern and the Co-Op and the tennis courts and took a left into the campsite, where we stepped into the office to pay the young woman in the bikini top, daughter of the husband and wife team who ran the place. I thought of how in another life I'd ask her out for a drink, but there was Cho at home and I missed her already and she was more than all of this. We parked the car by a picnic bench and put our tents up surrounding it and then we all headed off to the bus stop. At the bus stop I saw they'd reduced the bus timetable somewhat. I could see Scoie and Shackie, all knackered from the drive and all their years working, and the heat blazing down and as we waited for the bus I said, 'balls to it.' I'd been up Goatfell enough and we went back to the campsite and dropped off our rucksacks and came back out and went straight in The Pierhead, to watch football and drink beer. After a bit we went outside and saw gannets diving for fish in the bay.

I recognized the barmaid, young skinny lass off to Berlin after three years, we talked of the pool table, gone now, and how other things had changed, so she said. They didn't let them stay after work and drink all night any more, ploughing their wages back into the profits. I could see the thrill in her face at the chance of escape, and I hoped Berlin would be worth it for her. She finished her fag and went back to work, and we sat there, still in the shade but with the cooling breeze off the bay, the sand-filled playground opposite partly obscuring our view, and people on holiday walking up and down with prams and strollers and kids in tow, tattooed Glaswegians, some with beer cans, beer swilling blokes much like us, and then a few of the other Mancs turned up. They were staying the week, not just a night like us, and there was Sally Cox with her 'CUNT' t-shirt and Velvet Underground boyfriend. Then there was Martin, originally from Galway, and his old flame Nuala, and we had some pints with them and they told us Ron and Bill were still on their way, so we said we'd see them later as they still hadn't unpacked. We walked over the road to The Drift, all packed out with noisy families chomping on food, and the strange thing was they didn't sell the beer from the Arran brewery and even slagged it off, but we got cold blonde ales of some other kind anyway and sat in the beer garden sun just staring at the view and drinking and not needing to say anything as boats drifted across the bay and the gannets continued to dive. Minutes moved into hours as I nodded to myself in my knowledge of this good place and it was now that the beer began to take hold. I brought three pints sloshing back from the bar, lowered the pints to the table, licked the dripped beer off my fingers. I looked through the heat haze and my blurring eyes and smiled at the sight of the anchored tanker in the bay. Then I had a text that Ron and Bill had finally arrived after train problems at Preston. We got up and walked the shoreline road back to the Lamlash Bay Hotel, perhaps the best of the pubs on the island, with the same grizzled sozzlers on the same stools year after year – one guy his hair and beard just longer – and him with the same dry quips, the jibes about tourists. And the barmaids were the same as before too, just older and less innocent. Ron and Bill were sat in hats on chairs outside as the sun lowered, got more orange, covered them in that light, and I greeted them with a few sarky comments. Moose was there too, the big lad from Canada, and he gave me a rib-tickling hug and he was a great guy, great poet, Lorca fan, and someone got the beers in, probably not me as I'd pissed quite a few quid up the wall already. Later we went inside among the old soaks at the bar and Shackie and Scoie chatted with Ron and Bill and Moose, and Hannah Mercy was there too, the Norwich poet based in Manc who drank everyone under the table, and it was just beer after beer as the sun went down. Scoie and Shackie headed back to the campsite and left me there with Ron and Bill and Moose and Hannah and the guys at the bar and the barmaids, and I remember it getting blurry and saying 'yes' and feeling emotional when Ron asked me if I really loved Cho.

I woke at six, the sun burning its bright light through the tent walls and into my squinting eyes. The heat hit my beer thickened head, and as Scoie and Shackie went off for a cooked breakfast I lay on my camping mat in the shade of Shackie's car, blinking behind shades, trying not to vomit, watching as an old couple faffed about with an awning on their camper van.

Back at the call centre, I saw Connor from the agency and one of the managers, Wendy, approaching my desk. With smiling faces, they led me into the office.

'How has it been going so far?' asked Wendy, as Connor grinned.

'Okay.'

'You are happy with the role?'

'Yes.'

'Nothing we can help you with?'

'No, don't think so.'

'Okay well, you know that we are both here for you if you want to talk about anything, anything at all.'

'Okay.'

'Now, you were off on Saturday. Why didn't you phone in?'

'I did.'

'Who did you speak to?'

'I forget her name. But I told her to tell you I wouldn't be in.'

'Well you aren't supposed to leave a message. If you can't get through you need to try the other phone numbers.'

'I did get through.'

'Okay, I'm not going to argue with you about that.'

'Who is arguing?'

'So, you are better now?'

'Yep.'

'Can I ask what was wrong?'

'Man flu.'

'So, man flu on Saturday and after two days you are fine?'

'That's right, yes. It is not like I'm getting paid for Saturday is it?'

'Well, like I say, this is your back to work interview, so we just need to do this. Obviously, like you say, you don't get paid for sickness absence, but try to make sure that you speak to someone on the phone next time, okay?'

'Right.'

'Is there a problem?' asked Connor.

'Nope.'

'Then why are you shaking your head?'

'Well, I explained everything on the phone, and then I told you when I came in why I was off. Now I'm having to explain again.'

'It's just procedure. You aren't being singled out,' said Wendy.

I went back to my desk, clipped on the headphones and logged into the system. Almost immediately I heard the beep.

'Good morning, how can I help?' I asked, as Wendy came over and listened in on the call.

'Good morning. I would like to order a parasol please.'

'Okay. Do you know the product code?'

'Product code? Where would that be?'

'Just where it says product information. If you click on that.'

'Oh, I can't be bothered with that. It is a Marseille, eight seats. Table and chairs with parasol.'

'Okay, let's have a look.' I searched on the system and found it. 'Okay so that's the LG Outdoor Marseille. Eight-seater oval garden table and chairs set with parasol. Natural.'

'Sounds like it.'

'Two thousand, three hundred and ninety-nine pounds.'

'Yes, that's the one.'

'Okay can I just take your email address please?'

He gave me his email and I found him on the system, then asked him to confirm his address and postcode.

'When will it be delivered?' he asked.

'Standard delivery within fourteen days.'

'Oh. Fourteen days? I need it for Saturday.'

'It is because this item gets delivered from the supplier. Not by us. But they will contact you directly.'

'But I need it for Saturday.'

'I'm sorry about that.'

'Well I thought your company was supposed to be all about the great customer service?'

'We do our best.'

'You do your best? I need the parasol for Saturday. This is a joke.'

'I'm afraid we aren't able to do that with this item.'

'I've been a customer with you for many years. I've spent many thousands of pounds with you. I deserve better treatment than this.'

'I can put you through to a manager, if you like?' I said, looking over at Wendy who was avoiding eye contact. 'But like I say, the system won't allow me to do anything else.'

'Oh, forget it. Just forget it. I don't have time. I will go somewhere else. But I shall be registering my displeasure.'

'Okay. There's a section on the website where you can do that,' I said.

'Yes, yes, I'm well aware of that, and I will be, make no mistake.'

'Okay.'

'Okay.'

'Bye now.'

As I finished the call I looked at Wendy.

'How do you think that call went?' she asked.

'I think it went okay.'

'Yes, it was, I think it was *okay*, but there's things you should be saying. Like for example at the end you should be saying, is there anything else I can help you with? Anyway, you will be getting regular training updates, all being well. There is just one more thing for now though, and it is quite important. Do you think you could be just a little bit more *enthusiastic*?'

'Yeah,' I said, before she shuffled away.

Soon enough another call came through.

'Hello?' she said.

'Hello, how can I help?'

'Where have I got through to here?'

'This is the order line, in Manchester.'

'Thought I recognised the accent. Can I order something with you then?'

'Yes of course.'

'I'm from Bolton originally, but I'm in Devon now.'

'Oh right. Better weather down there.'

'Oh yes, miles better. I wouldn't want to be back in Bolton now . . . stop nudging me will you, I'm on the phone. Sorry, that's me husband. He's too shy, aren't you, love? Won't come on the phone.'

'What is it you would like to order?'

'Lawnmower. One of them remote control ones.'

'Do you know the product code?'

'Zero two four, eight six eight seven three.'

'That's the Ambrogio, Elie S Plus.'

'That's it. Red one.'

It cost over three grand. I took her details and put the payment through.

'Birthday present for him,' she said. 'Lazy sod can't mow the lawn himself anymore.'

'You must have a big lawn,' I said. 'I'm in a flat, don't even have a garden.'

'Of course you don't. Yes, we've got acres. It's a long way from Bromley Cross, I'm telling you. Have you been there?'

'Don't think so.'

'Kind of on the way to Blackburn out of Bolton. It was okay back then. Anyway, I wouldn't swap places now. Thanks then.'

'Bye now.'

I turned around and saw Wendy looking at me from her desk. She shook her head, had another crisp, drank some more pop.

When I got back to Manchester there was a reading organized in Didsbury, as part of their arts festival. Unlike nearby Chorlton their arts festival wasn't a shambles and you did actually get paid if you performed. I'd had a call about it before I went to Arran, from someone at the festival who asked if I could put her in touch with the other Manchester writers living there. I gave her a few phone numbers and then the next thing I knew about it was a post on Facebook, plugging the event.

It was short stories by Manchester writers, and there were five writers performing. Despite the fact that I was actually from Manchester, unlike some on the bill, and had been in Best British Short Stories three times, and had several collections of short fiction published, had also lived in Didsbury on and off for a number of years, and on top of that had even helped the organizers to get the ball rolling, I wasn't invited to read. Around that time a short story anthology came out where the writers had been asked to write stories based on paintings. I'd done a whole book on that. It was easy to see how writers could get bitter. Sometimes I wondered if I even existed, and what the point was of all the unpaid hours I spent writing. I realized that just because you fitted the bill, it didn't mean you got on the bill, just because you came from somewhere it didn't mean anything. The Manchester Literature Festival, for example. You could count the Manchester writers who had ever appeared there on the fingers of one hand. But I hadn't read Graham Norton's novel, maybe it was amazing.

One morning I got a call from the agency to say that I was no longer required at The Flowers business park. It seemed that my burgeoning call centre career had come to a premature end.

The rest of the summer I lived off my savings. Since moving in with Cho I could no longer claim Universal Credit. She was too proud to, and you couldn't live in the same place with one person making a claim and the other not. So, I stayed at home, guilt free, reading books, or writing, in the morning, and just poncing around Heaton Moor in the afternoon.

When September came around I looked for more Learning Support work and the agency found me a job at a college in Rochdale. Rochdale, home of grooming gangs and Cyril

Smith. They had had the good sense to strip him of his honours. I had to get a train, a tram and a bus to get there, and it took me the best part of two hours. But I had all of John Fante's novels on my Kindle and the time passed. At the end of the first day I had been reading *1933 Was A Bad Year*, on the bus home. A very short novel that contains Fante's very best writing, all about a young lad who wants to be a baseball player and avoid becoming a bricklayer like his father.

I got off the bus at Shudehill and instead of getting the tram across town I walked it to Piccadilly Station the back way. The sun was shining on a big pile of rubble cordoned off by metal fences. They were knocking red brick buildings down in the Northern Quarter. I carried on through what looked like a film set, and around the corner they were actually filming something. One of those TV dramas filled with working class clichés. I had never really known this part of town and walking through it felt like being in a different city.

At Piccadilly I waited for the train. It was twenty minutes late, the usual scenario. Another Northern Rail fail. It was hard to believe how so much money filtered through the hands of a company so obviously inept. As the crappy old train crawled to a halt we all piled on. As it tried to set off again the driver couldn't get it to start for another ten minutes. People all around me were sighing and grumbling and sweating. The carriage I got on was near the toilet and when the door opened it stank of thirty years of piss. Every time the train jolted across points the guy next to me banged his rucksack into my shoulder. Almost everyone looked at their phones. Sunlight filtered in through the windows and I glanced across to the see the Etihad shimmering in the distance. People got off at Levenshulme and it was slightly easier to breathe. Soon there was the lovely chocolate smell as we passed by the back of the McVitie's factory before slowing into Heaton Chapel.

We parked on Redruth Street just off Platt Lane and walked to the ground down alleys at the back of terraced houses and went into the Kippax through painted blue turnstiles. Dad would usually get a match programme from the stall and we'd walk up the stairs and in through the tunnel to stand about halfway up the Kippax and near the halfway line, but I don't remember if there was a programme for this particular game and I'm vague about the score, though I remember that City beat United, and there were eighteen thousand there for what was the Youth Cup Final.

There were youngsters playing who would go on to be the backbone of the first team: Andy Hinchcliffe, Steve Redmond, Ian Brightwell, Paul Moulden, Paul Lake, David White and Ian Scott. They were managed by Tony Book and Glyn Pardoe, a couple of great old players, and wore the best kit of all time, the one with Phillips on the front, quite a pale blue with a scratchy collar. Pardoe had been at the club for donkey's years, having made his debut as a boy of fifteen, and had to give up playing because of injury after an horrendous tackle by the great George Best.

Paul Lake got injured too, knackering his knee, and later wrote a splendid book called *I'm Not Really Here* that chronicled all the struggles he had. Lake, Hinchcliffe and White all played for England, but Whitie was me and Dad's favourite. There was even a book about that youth cup team called *Teenage Kicks*.

I remember one of Whitie's first appearances. It was during a phase I had of watching the game from the very bottom of the stand with Houghy, looking through the iron railings that got taken down after Hillsborough. Dad stayed in his usual spot halfway up the stand, with his mate from work, Terry, a little bloke with bow legs who chain-smoked B&H and wore a brown leather jacket. Whitie got the ball and knocked it past the full back and sprinted off. He had such pace. Sometimes he'd knock it too far, so that it went out for a goal kick before he had chance to cross it in, and he was raw like that to start with. But there was something about watching a youngster's debut, and my Dad loved that they were all local lads, it seemed to make it more meaningful to him.

When I made a splash for Audi Rovers, and got spotted by a City scout when I was playing for Tameside Boys, my Dad seemed a foot taller, stuck his chest out, I'm sure of it. It is a hard thing for me to admit, but I'm not sure I ever would have made it, even without the injury. It has taken me a long time to accept that. But it was the inspiration of lads like Lake and White that made me believe, that made my Dad believe back then. Though I never played for the first team I did still play for City, and nobody can ever take that away.

I don't know why City ever let Whitie go, because when he went to Leeds he still did well. Like Lake he had to retire because of injury in the end. At least he got six or seven more years than Lake. I remembered the highlights of Whitie's time at City. The hat-trick in the 10-1 game against Huddersfield, four goals in the game against Aston Villa, a couple against Liverpool, performances that earned him his one and only England cap. He got some stick after that England game because they said he missed a load of chances, but I don't remember it that way. He kept all his shots on target, but the keeper had a great game and saved them all. Whitie never played for England again.

When it came out about Barry Bennell abusing all the boys it was so sad to find out that Whitie was among them. That it had happened to my favourite player seemed to bring the horror of it even closer. But he was doing something about it, he'd gone public. I followed him on Twitter, listened to him during his occasional appearances on Radio XFM Manchester with Ian Cheeseman.

He wrote an autobiography called *Shades of Blue*, and he was plugging it on Twitter when it came out. It didn't get much publicity because of the Bennell case. He was offering a ten percent discount, and I direct messaged him on Twitter. We sorted my payment and address details, and he said he'd try and get the book out to me as soon as he could.

A week or so later the bell rang. I went to the front door and there was a tall bloke standing there, grey hair, grey stubble, bit of a belly on him. It was only when he held out the book that I realised it was Whitie. I got a selfie with him and he said he had loads more to deliver, so I didn't get chance to say anything to him about what a great player he'd been, what a legend of the club.

Whitie looked a bit like me, getting grey, getting heavy, a bit of timber around the belly. I'd try jogging, but like Whitie with his ankle, my knee injury would make it impossible. I thought of going swimming at Withington Baths.

Whitie was from the time when they didn't get all the money, not like now when a few week's wages for the top players could keep you financially secure forever. His dad had a scrap metal firm and they fell out because Whitie couldn't tell his dad about Bennell. The book was part of a recovery, but it was a celebration too, a celebration of goals and glory. Most of all it was about playing for City, and what a golden thing that was. He scored seventy-nine goals for the boys in blue.

The more I read *Shades of Blue*, like I'd read Lake's book *I'm Not Really Here*, I realised that though they were legends they were also just normal guys from Manchester. You played the games you played, good and bad, and it lasted as long as it lasted, and though there was a void there after, a void that would never go away, you just moved on, tried to get on with your life.

Sometimes they must lie there in bed and think of the good times, the times when it felt like the pitch was their own, and nobody else on that day was as good as they were. For me, it was the game when I scored six for Audi Rovers. There's great solace in the memory of those goals. Another one I remember was scored on the fields in Audenshaw where I played so often with my mate Houghy, right near where he died on the astro-turf cricket pitch. It was around the time the council had planted some new trees. Dad crossed the ball. It came over my shoulder and I connected perfectly with it. I think about that even now, as the trees sway high above the grass.

Acknowledgements

THANKS ONCE AGAIN to Chris, Jen and Nick at Salt. Thanks also to David White for his inspiring autobiography *Shades of Blue*.

This book has been typeset by
SALT PUBLISHING LIMITED
using Neacademia, a font designed by Sergei Egorov
for the Rosetta Type Foundry in the Czech Republic. It
is manufactured using Holmen Book Cream 70gsm, a
Forest Stewardship Council™ certified paper from the
Hallsta Paper Mill in Sweden. It was printed and bound
by Clays Limited in Bungay, Suffolk, Great Britain.

CROMER
GREAT BRITAIN
MMXIX